The sharp blac
with a glare.

'It would be as well
it would also be as w~~~~ you to bear in mind
that within the walls of this palace and the
grounds that surround it every single thing,
without exception, belongs to me.'

Amber responded in a tight tone. 'I'll bear that
in mind. From now on, I'll take great care to
treat your possessions with the utmost respect.
Just as I'm sure,' she added cuttingly, 'you
treat them yourself.'

Plainly amused by her rebuke, he raised one
black eyebrow, as cruel as the curve of a
hawk's wing, and informed her, 'Perhaps I
ought to clarify something... My personal
philosophy regarding my possessions could be
described less as the belief that they are there
to receive my respect and rather more as the
conviction that their purpose is to serve me.'

He paused before adding with a cool, predatory smile, 'And to provide me with pleasure—
whenever and however I may wish it.'

Stephanie Howard was born and brought up in Dundee in Scotland, and educated at the London School of Economics. For ten years she worked as a journalist in London on a variety of women's magazines, among them *Woman's Own*, and was latterly editor of the now-defunct *Honey*. She has spent many years living and working abroad—in Italy, Malaysia, the Philippines and in the Middle East.

Recent titles by the same author:

THE DUKE'S WIFE
THE LADY'S MAN
THE COLORADO COUNTESS

AMBER AND THE SHEIKH

BY

STEPHANIE HOWARD

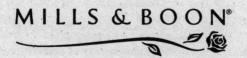

MILLS & BOON and MILLS & BOON with the Rose Device are registered trademarks of the publisher.

First published in Great Britain 1997
Harlequin Mills & Boon Limited,
Eton House, 18–24 Paradise Road, Richmond, Surrey TW9 1SR

© Stephanie Howard 1997

ISBN 0 263 80072 5

Set in 10 on 12 pt Linotron Times
02-9704-52589-D

Typeset in Great Britain by CentraCet, Cambridge
Printed and bound in Great Britain
by Mackays of Chatham PLC, Chatham

CHAPTER ONE

A PAIR of eyes, as black as whirlpools, swept across the shimmering desert landscape and came to rest on the figure of a slim, blonde-haired girl.

Instantly, the black eyes narrowed and, beneath the long white Arab robes, every muscle in the whiplash-hard body stiffened. Was he seeing things? Surely, he must be? This must be some kind of mirage. It was too much to hope that such a prize had come his way.

Impatiently, he reached for the field-glasses round his neck. It had often been said—and not just by those who wished to flatter him—that he was gifted with the clear, uncanny vision of a hawk, but from this distance it was possible that his eyes had deceived him. The sand-dune on whose sharply sculpted summit he stood was a good two hundred metres from the Bedouin encampment where he had spotted her. More than likely, what he had seen had indeed been a mirage, for the blinding desert light could so easily play tricks.

Frowning, his body tense, he raised the glasses and carefully focused.

The untidy huddle of ragged brown tents instantly jumped up to meet him, so close that he could make out in every tiny detail the grubby, laughing faces of a group of children playing in the dust. He swung the glasses round, past a pair of tethered camels, past a group of old men squatting in the shade, past a black-veiled woman bent over her cooking pots. And he cursed to himself. So he had just been seeing things. He might have known such a miracle could not possibly be.

But then, as he continued to search through the jumble of tents, like a flower springing out of the sand suddenly there she was again.

'*Wallahi!*'

He felt his heart thrust triumphantly against his ribs. So his eyes, after all, had not deceived him! This glorious vision was no figment of his imagination!

Very still, scarcely believing his good fortune, he studied her.

She was standing talking to two men, one a Bedouin elder, the other, at a guess, a local interpreter. And, as he watched her, he felt a clench of fierce excitement. This really was a miracle. He had dreamed of a girl like this.

He let his gaze flow over her lithe, shapely figure— slim, but not too slim, like so many Western women— dressed in beige cotton trousers and a baggy white shirt. Then his eyes moved to her face, which he also found pleasing. Heart-shaped. Blue-eyed. Full of life and sparkle as she leaned to say something to the Bedouin elder and laughed.

But the hair, a shoulder-length cloud of honey-blonde curls, was by far the most pleasing attribute of all. She was the answer to his prayers. His dreams made flesh and bone.

A smile touched his lips as excitement flared inside him. Now that he had found her, he knew what he must do.

Lowering his field-glasses, he turned to his companion, a tall man, though half a head shorter than himself, with a thick black beard and bright, clever eyes, who had been standing quietly at his side.

'Rashid, there's a girl down there in the camp. A European girl. Blonde and very beautiful.' As he spoke, he slipped the field-glasses from around his neck and handed them to the other man, inviting him to take a look. He smiled. 'She is to be the one. Kindly arrange it.'

Having given the order, he turned away abruptly and, informed by some sixth sense, glanced up into the sky, where a shadow had appeared against the diamond-bright sun.

'Come!' he commanded, holding out his wrist, protected by its thick leather falconer's gauntlet. And, instantly, on obedient golden wings, the falcon dropped from the sky to perch there without a sound.

'Good girl,' he murmured, lightly stroking the fierce head, as the bright yellow eyes met his, unblinking. And as he reached into his pocket for the bird's leather hood and slipped it over the glossy feathered head he smiled to himself with warm satisfaction. They had caught nothing today, but still it had been a good day's hunting. Within his grasp had unexpectedly strayed a truly priceless prize.

Still smiling to himself, he headed quickly down the sand-dune to where a dusty blue Range Rover was waiting in the shade. As he moved, the edges of his white *kaffiyeh*, the traditional Arab headdress, secured by its black silk cord, fluttered back to reveal his face.

Strikingly masculine. Full of sensuality and power. The deep-set black eyes shrewd and intelligent and fringed with the kind of lashes most women would die for. Proud, arrogant nose. Wide, masterful mouth. It was a face that in the course of its owner's thirty-four years had sent many different kinds of shivers down many different spines.

As he reached the car, he turned briefly to Rashid, his servant, who had followed.

'See to the girl at once,' he commanded. 'Don't waste any time.'

Rashid nodded. 'Have no fear, my lord. The deed will be done at once.' He was already plotting how best to carry out this new task, never considering for one moment that it might prove to be impossible.

For Sheikh Zoltan bin Hamad al-Khalifa had spoken. And whatever Sheikh Zoltan decreed must be done.

'Don, this place is magic. Unlike anywhere I've ever been. Now I know what people actually mean when they talk about the mysterious allure of the Orient!'

Amber Buchanan, dressed in a bright turquoise kaftan and seated cross-legged on the blue coverlet of her hotel bed, positively glowed with enthusiasm as she spoke into the phone.

'There's only one problem.' A frown briefly creased her brow as she shook back her cloud of blonde hair. 'Those interviews I lined up before I left London... Half of them have been cancelled. Just like that, no reason given. And my trip to the Bedouin camp this morning turned out to be a total waste of time. They just didn't want to co-operate at all.'

She sighed. 'Somehow I'm going to have to find a way to win them round.'

There was a warm, knowing laugh at the other end of the line. 'Well, I don't reckon that ought to pose too much of a problem.'

For Don, her partner in Ambra Research, the company she'd set up three years ago at the age of twenty-three, was well aware of Amber's powers of persuasion. 'She could charm the hind legs off a donkey,' he'd often been heard to say.

He asked her now, 'So do you reckon you'll still be able to make it back here by the end of next week?'

'I'll move heaven and earth, Don. But I'll let you know for sure in a couple of days. I'll fax you. Can you hang on till then?'

'No problem. I'll wait to hear from you, then. And now I'd better go. While you're lazing about beneath the palm trees, some of us have got to work,' he joked.

Amber laughed. 'My heart weeps for you.' Then, wickedly, she added, 'I'll think of you out in the February drizzle while I'm sipping my orange juice by the pool.'

'Sadist! Bye, Amber.'

'Bye, Don. I'll be in touch.'

Amber was smiling as she laid the phone down and leaned back against the pillows. Orange juice by the pool! Chance would be a fine thing! Since she'd arrived here, just over forty-eight hours ago, in the fabulously wealthy little desert sheikhdom of Ras al-Houht, she'd been running around like something possessed. She didn't even know where the hotel pool was!

She'd come to Ras al-Houht to do some research for her novelist mother, who was writing a book set in the area—a highly unlikely tale, in Amber's opinion, about an English girl who got captured by a band of Bedouin and ended up falling in love with their leader! As Amber had pointed out, girls these days really didn't go for that macho type of hero. Though her opinion, needless to say, had fallen on deaf ears as her mother had simply responded with one of her 'I know better' smiles!

Amber was actually extremely glad her mother had stuck to her guns, for she'd been looking forward immensely to this trip to Arabia. For one thing, she'd never visited this part of the world before, and, for another, it would provide a very welcome break—her first since ending her engagement to Adrian six months ago.

That had been a devastating business, painful and messy, and it had profoundly shocked her family and friends, for during their two and half years together everyone had always said that she and Adrian were a perfect couple. Even now, Amber often sensed that some of them still thought she'd been mad to give him up.

All in all, it had been a miserable, stressful six months and she'd welcomed the chance to get away from London for a couple of weeks and spend some time in a totally different environment—especially since she'd be doing what she enjoyed most, namely her beloved research. Though, in fact, as she'd just been explaining to Don, now that she was here she was actually getting very little research done!

It was maddening and frustrating and she was going to have to do something about it, for if she wasn't back in the office next week to hold the fort Don would be forced to postpone his trip to California. But what exactly ought she to do? That was the problem.

With a frown she let her gaze drift out through the open window to the view of graceful palm trees against a vivid sapphire sky with the pale, shimmering outline of a minaret in the distance. She found this place fascinating and far more beautiful than she'd expected, but at the same time she was growing more and more aware that things just didn't work the way they did in the West.

Her irritation at the cancelled interviews and her efforts to change people's minds had been met with a shrug and a shake of the head. What she needed was a new approach and perhaps someone to give her a few clues about how to get inside the Arab psyche!

At that very moment, there was a knock on the door.

'Just a minute! I'm coming!'

Amber smiled to herself as she jumped down from the bed and hurried to answer it. Maybe someone up there had been moved by her dilemma and this was a messenger with the solution to all her problems— though it was probably only Room Service delivering fresh towels!

It wasn't Room Service, however. It was one of the young men from Reception

'This is for you,' he told her, handing her an envelope. 'It was delivered by hand just a couple of minutes ago.'

'Thank you '

Amber took the envelope, frowning at it curiously. It looked terribly important—in heavy cream vellum, with her name, Miss Amber Buchanan, written most artistically on the front. On the back, as she could see as she turned it over, was an elaborate gold-embossed insignia in Arabic. Her curiosity quadrupled. Who on earth could it be from?

She gave the young man a tip and closed the bedroom door again. Then, impatiently, she tore the envelope open and pulled out the single sheet of paper it contained. On it was written the most astonishing message.

Amber read it and blinked.

Then she read it again.

> Sheikh Zoltan bin Hamad al-Khalifa, Emir of the Princely State of Ras al-Houht, requests your presence at the Emiri Palace at ten o' clock tomorrow morning.

She raised her blue eyes and laughed with delight. Well, how about that! Perhaps she'd been right, after all! Maybe someone up there really had decided to help her!

Next morning, at three minutes to ten precisely, Amber's taxi swept through the gilded gates of the Emiri Palace, a vast, shimmering edifice in ice-white marble, all glittering spires, gilded domes and gleaming turrets, set amidst acres of ornamental gardens and guarded from the flat, burning desert that surrounded it by an outer boundary of high stone walls.

As she peered through the taxi window, Amber was burning with excitement. In the course of her career as a freelance researcher she'd met all sorts of powerful and important people—diplomats, politicians, even a couple of heads of state—but she'd never come face to face with a real Arab sheikh. And her mother would be thrilled at this unexpected development, for who knew what interesting little nuggets of information she might pick up in the course of her visit to the palace?

Naturally, she was wondering why the sheikh had invited her, but the more she thought about it, the more likely it seemed that he'd simply heard of her visit to his country—probably via the Ministry of Information, from whom she'd had to get permission to do her research and who'd also fixed up most of her interviews for her, though they'd just shrugged when the interviews had fallen through!—and was merely interested to find out more about what she was here for. In a small place like this that wouldn't be so unusual.

And his curiosity could turn out to be a bit of luck for her.

Maybe, if she played her cards right, he might be disposed to use his influence to help!

At the rear entrance to the palace, where the taxi finally set her down, a tall black-bearded man was waiting for her.

'Rashid,' he introduced himself, bowing deeply. 'At your service.'

Amber had to struggle to hold back a smile. Was this for real or had she stepped into some *Arabian Nights*-type movie? 'Pleased to meet you,' she told him, resisting the temptation to point out that there was really no need for all this deference and formality. She was just an ordinary working English girl. No better than him.

Rashid led her inside the palace, across a vast, glittering hallway hung with glorious brass lanterns and strewn with priceless silk rugs, to a large, bright reception room, whose tall arched doorway was flanked by a pair of moustached and turbaned guards, each with a bejewelled, glittering scabbard at his waist.

Amber glanced at them. Did they ever actually use these fancy swords? Maybe they came in handy for trimming their toenails!

With a polite wave of his hand, Rashid bade her take

a seat. 'His Highness will meet you here,' he told her as she made herself comfortable on one of the high-backed chairs. Then, with another deep bow, he turned and vanished from the room, like a genie disappearing back inside his magic lamp.

Left alone, Amber had a good look round her. The room was exquisite, decorated in rich, deep colours, with soft-looking divans and chairs with high carved backs arranged invitingly against the walls. So this, she thought with a smile, was how Arab sheikhs lived. Though this room, of course, would only be the *diwan*, the place where, according to tradition, guests were received. Heaven knew what his private quarters were like!

She was absolutely dying to meet the owner of all this luxury. Last night, she'd spent a couple of hours at the hotel going through a pile of local English-language newspapers, studying the sheikh's photographs and trying to find out all she could about him. But, though there were plenty of reports on his various business and political manoeuvres—from which it was clear he was a shrewd and intelligent man—she'd found nothing at all on a personal level. There hadn't even been any clue as to whether or not he was married—though he undoubtedly was, of course, with a whole harem of wives!

All this was going through her head as she glanced admiringly round the room and suddenly spied a pair of half-open French windows, which appeared to lead out into a shady courtyard.

On an impulse, she left her seat and stepped towards them. She'd have plenty of time to take a quick peek outside. VIPs, in her experience, invariably showed up late for appointment. Pushing the doors open, she stepped outside—and let out a gasp of sheer delight.

In the centre of the courtyard, which was green with potted palms, was a pretty marble fountain in the shape of three entwined dolphins, from whose grinning, upturned mouths spouted a triple rain of water that sparkled like liquid crystal in the softly dappled light. And in a corner by a pot of deep pink flowering cactus, tail fanned out behind him, strutted a magnificent snow-white peacock.

Amber reached in her bag for the camera she always carried with her. This was pure magic! Definitely worth a photograph!

'I think not, Miss Buchanan. Please put the camera away.' Before she even had time to focus, a harsh male voice behind her spoke.

Amber whirled round, startled, colour flying to her cheeks, and found herself looking into a pair of narrowed eyes, as black as whirlpools and twice as deadly as sin.

CHAPTER TWO

BEFORE Amber could say a word, he elaborated in a cutting tone, 'This is not the Pyramids of Giza, Miss Buchanan. This is private property, not some tourist attraction. We do not encourage the taking of photographs.'

'I'm sorry.'

Amber had difficulty getting the words out. The force of those dark eyes seemed to have paralysed her momentarily. Her skin prickled strangely as she looked into his face.

She knew who he was, of course. She recognised him from his photographs. The tall, imposing figure standing in the doorway was, without a doubt, Sheikh Zoltan, her host. But, though he resembled his photographs, the photographs had deceived her, for in no way had they prepared her for the flesh-and-blood reality of the man.

As he stepped from the doorway and came unhurriedly towards her, the fine white *kaffiyeh* fluttering back from his face, it was all Amber could do not to flinch away from him. This man possessed a power that seemed to reach out and take hold of her. She could feel it close around her like fingers of steel that might squeeze from her every ounce of resistance she possessed.

It was the strangest sensation, like nothing she'd ever known. Unnerving, and yet, as the fighting adrenalin rushed through her, unexpectedly exciting at the same time.

There was another quality, too, that the photographs had failed to warn her of. From every sinew and pore he oozed sexuality. It was in the set of his bold features, in the way he moved and held himself, in the fierce, intense way the fathomless black eyes looked at her. Everything about him proclaimed that here was a man whose natural habitat was the shadowy world of the senses. A sexual being to his fingertips. Virile and predatory.

Deep down inside her, she was aware of something responding. An involuntary, visceral tingling in her blood. It took a surprising, and slightly alarming, amount of will-power to crush it.

He came to a halt just a couple of metres away. 'Is it your custom,' he demanded in that voice as harsh as sandpaper, 'to treat the property of others with such casual disrespect? If it is, I would advise you to change your ways rather quickly. It is not the way we do things around here.'

'I'm sorry,' Amber said again. 'But really I meant no disrespect.'

She felt about half an inch tall, like a child caught misbehaving, though at the same time she had to fight an almost overwhelming impulse to tell him he was overreacting. She'd only been about to take a photograph, for heaven's sake. She hadn't been daubing graffiti on the palace wall!

But she bit back the urge. It was his palace, after all, and he was the Emir of Ras al-Houht, and that pretty much gave him the right to react any way he liked! Besides, it would be silly to risk getting into a fight with him. She was hoping to persuade him to help her, after all. Much better to make an effort to try and win him round.

She tried a tentative smile. 'Believe me,' she assured him, 'I didn't mean to treat your palace like a tourist attraction. It's just that this little courtyard, with the peacock and everything, is so beautiful that I suddenly wanted to take a photograph. I didn't think what I was doing. It was an impulse, really.'

'An impulse. I see.'

There was no softening in the black eyes. Hard and unblinking, they continued to watch her, travelling over her face in its frame of soft blonde hair, seeming to examine every detail with close attention—the wide blue eyes, the creamy pale skin, warmed now by two bright spots of colour, the soft, vulnerable lips, where his gaze lingered for a moment with an intimacy that almost made her feel as though he'd touched her.

'There are certain impulses, Miss Buchanan, which one must learn to control. Particularly those impulses concerning the property of others.'

'Yes, I know, but—'

He continued, as though she hadn't spoken. 'Most men, when it comes to their personal property, are notoriously protective and jealous, I find, and in this I am no different from anyone else.' He paused. 'You might even say I am more protective and jealous than most. I allow no one to take liberties with or tamper with what is mine.'

The sharp black eyes fixed her with a glare. 'It would be as well for you to know this. And it would also be as well for you to bear in mind that within the walls of this palace and the grounds that surround it every single thing, without exception, belongs to me.'

As he spoke, with what looked like deliberate provocation, the intense dark gaze flowed down from her
face, examining and absorbing every square inch of her
physique. The generous swell of her bosom, the neat
waist, the flaring hips. And what he was seeing, it
seemed to Amber, was not her long-sleeved cotton
blouse, nor the narrow blue-checked skirt that reached
well below her knees—for she was dressed with careful
respect for the customs of the country—what he was
seeing was the warm, scented, feminine flesh beneath.

Damned cheek! What did he think she was? Some
recruit to his harem? It had felt almost as though he was
ravishing her on the spot! Well, maybe everything in the
palace and the grounds belonged to him, but that most
definitely did not include her!

Reining back the impulse to point this out to him, she
flashed him a disapproving look and responded in a
tight tone, 'I'll bear that in mind. From now on, I shall
take great care to treat your possessions with the utmost
respect. Just as, I'm sure,' she added cuttingly, 'you treat
them yourself.'

Her expression and tone of voice very clearly con-
veyed that the 'possessions' she was referring to were
the women in his life—for, of course, mere possessions
was all they would be to him—and that she was actually
very certain he showed them no respect at all. The man
was a male chauvinist through to his bones!

It was quite obvious he'd understood and he made no
effort to disagree. Plainly amused by her rebuke, he
raised one black eyebrow, as cruel as the curve of a
hawk's wing, and informed her, 'I take due note of your
judgement, Miss Buchanan, but perhaps I ought to
clarify something... My personal philosophy regarding

my possessions could be described less as the belief that they are there to receive my respect and rather more as the conviction that their purpose is to serve me.'

He paused before adding with a cool, predatory smile, 'And to provide me with pleasure—whenever and however I may wish it.'

As his eyes impaled her, something inside Amber shivered. That remark had sounded alarmingly like a warning. Then as he raised one long-fingered, olive-skinned hand, as though he was about to reach out and touch her, again she had to fight not to flinch back from him. But he did not touch her. Instead, with a deft movement he flicked the white *kaffiyeh* back over his shoulders, revealing a glimpse of the coal-black hair that curled around his ears.

Then he was turning away. 'Let us go indoors,' he commanded. And he proceeded on swift strides to lead her across the courtyard, past the sun-dappled fountain, through a high arched doorway and into a maze of narrow, unlit corridors that seemed to be taking them into the very bowels of the palace, till, at last, at the foot of a winding flight of stairs, they were stepping into a shadowy, sandalwood-scented room where low divans, scattered with cushions, lined the crimson-dark, silk-covered walls.

A cursory wave of the hand. 'Take a seat,' he instructed. Then he waited till she'd done so before seating himself opposite her, his movements as supple and as graceful as a cat's.

Against the braided and tasselled cushions he presented an exotically dramatic picture. The stark white of his robes. The fierce black of his hair and eyes. Amber looked at him, her brain suddenly whirring with questions. Why had he brought her to this hidden-away corner of the palace? What was on his mind? Why had he invited her here at all?

Suddenly, for the first time since she'd received his invitation, she was aware of a flicker of apprehension in her heart.

He was glancing across at her. 'I expect you would like some tea?'

'Oh, don't bother about tea.'

She knew that was discourteous, but all at once an alarm bell was ringing in her head. There was something not quite right here. It might be wiser not to linger, just to get down to whatever business he'd brought her here to talk about and then be gone as quickly as she could. She was searching for a diplomatic way of putting this to him when she sensed that someone had entered the room.

Startled, she spun round. In fact, two men had appeared, both clearly servants, dressed in blue robes and turbans, each carrying an enormous beaten brass tray, one laden with a tea-service in lavishly gold leafed porcelain, the other with silver dishes on which were artistically arranged a mouth-watering array of sweet-meats and cakes. Little date and nut clusters, tiny choux pastries, almond-scented *goriba*, bite-sized *konafa*, dripping with honey.

Amber watched in dismay, feeling as though a wall was closing round her, as the servants proceeded to lay out this astonishing mini-banquet on the low brass table that stood between her and the Sheikh. How on earth was she going to manage a speedy escape now if she was expected to wade her way through all this?

But she had to. Something close to panic was flicker-

ing inside her as she could feel, as sharp as a knife
against her flesh, the unwavering black gaze still fixed
upon her.

Abruptly, she turned to face him again, feeling a
shiver race down her spine as she looked into the
intense, unblinking eyes.

'This looks absolutely lovely,' she said, referring to
the food and having to fight rather hard to keep her
tone light. 'But you really shouldn't have gone to so
much trouble. I only had breakfast a short while ago
and I couldn't eat a thing.'

She smiled apologetically. 'Besides, I'm aware that
you must be an extremely busy man with far more
important things to do than sit around having tea. So I
wouldn't mind in the least if we just skipped all this and
got straight down to discussing whatever it was you
wanted to see me about. Then I can get off back to my
hotel and out of your way.'

Amber could feel her heart thudding against her ribs
as she spoke and her hands were clenched into tight,
nervous fists. That look in his eyes wasn't just idle
curiosity. And neither was it harmless sexual interest.
There was more to it than that. She was becoming more
and more convinced of it. He hadn't just brought her
here to find out about her research. Behind that brood-
ing gaze, Sheikh Zoltan was plotting something.

She thought back in alarm to the baffling maze of
corridors that he'd led her along to get to this room. If
she had to escape, she'd never find her way back.

And those guards with their fancy swords... Maybe
they *did* use them, after all!

The dark eyes continued to fix her for a moment.
Then he smiled. 'That is most thoughtful of you. I

appreciate your concern. And, of course, you are quite right. It is not my custom to waste time.'

His tone was suddenly lightened with an edge of dry humour, as though he found her protest amusing.

'However,' he continued, 'I never consider it a waste to take the time to observe the customs of my country and people, among the most important of which is the offering of hospitality to one's guests. So, my dear Miss Buchanan, you may put your mind at rest. In no way do I consider this encounter to be time wasted. On the contrary, I consider it to be time exceedingly well spent.'

As the two servants departed, having completed their task, right down to pouring out two cups of scented tea, he paused to wave an imperious hand over the array of dishes.

'Now please help yourself to something to eat.'

There was little choice but to obey. To go on insisting would appear strange. Besides, that quick smile and flash of dry humour had helped to ease her fears a little.

She was probably just being crazy. Who did she think she was, anyway? The dewy-eyed heroine of her mother's book, about to be kidnapped by the wild Bedouin chieftain? That was totally insane. This was Sheikh Zoltan, a sophisticated, civilised, educated man. In spite of the unnerving way he kept looking at her, it was hardly likely that he was about to throw her over his shoulder and carry her off like a prisoner to his harem. She was just letting her imagination run away with her.

Making a determined effort to force back her anxiety, Amber reached out and helped herself to a small pastry.

'Thank you,' she murmured, laying it on a gold-leafed plate, adding a slice of lemon to her tea and taking a small sip. Just calm down, she told herself, for her hands

were shaking a bit. I'm sure there's nothing to be
worried about.

Sheikh Zoltan had leaned forward to take a cake too.
Amber was careful not to look at him directly, for she
still felt uneasy about meeting that rapacious gaze, but
she could sense his every movement vividly as he bit
into it and took a mouthful of his tea. It felt rather like
being shut up in a cage with a tiger that you were
desperately trying to talk yourself into believing
wouldn't harm you!

Then suddenly he said, 'Very well, I'll get to the
point. Let me explain to you the reason why I invited
you here.'

He laid down his cup and touched a napkin to his lips,
as Amber held her breath and anxiously waited for him
to continue.

For better or worse, she was about to discover what
this was all about.

'I was curious to meet you,' he went on at last, 'after it
was brought to my attention that you've come to Ras al-
Houht in order to do some research for a book.' For the
first time, he smiled what could have been called a light,
informal smile. 'Naturally, I was curious, so I decided to
invite you here so that you could tell me more.'

Relief rushed through her like floodwater through a
breached dam. You're a lunatic, she told herself. What
in heaven's name came over you? You've been getting
yourself into a state about nothing!

She smiled back at him, trying not to grin like an
idiot. 'I'd be more than happy to tell you anything you
want to know.'

Sheikh Zoltan was leaning back against the cushions
of the divan. 'This research you've come to do. . .' His

expression had grown softer. 'I've been told you're doing it on behalf of your mother. She's a novelist, I understand, currently writing a book set in Ras al-Houht?'

Amber nodded in response. 'That's right,' she answered. She, too, relaxed back against her cushions as she spoke.

'So, you work for your mother?'

'Sometimes I do. I'm a freelance researcher. My partner and I get hired by all sorts of different people. Writers. Academics. Big companies. Small companies.' She smiled, unable to hide her satisfaction at the reputation she and Don had earned for themselves and that these days caused them to be very much in demand. 'Whatever information anyone needs, we can generally find a way to track it down for them.'

Sheikh Zoltan smiled. 'It sounds like an interesting job.'

'It's the most interesting job in the world. I absolutely love it.'

'Yes, I can see that.' His eyes scanned her face. Then he leaned forward a little, still smiling as he asked her, 'So, what sort of information have you come to Ras al-Houht to track down?'

This was the demand Amber had initially come here expecting, and on the way to the palace she'd carefully prepared her answer.

'Well,' she began, 'I need different kinds of information. General information about the history and social customs of the country, plus more specific, detailed information on what life is like in a Bedouin camp.'

'I see. Then you definitely need to do your research.

The Bedouin lifestyle is a very particular one. These days, even many Arabs whose roots are Bedouin but who now live in the city have forgotten about that old life.'

Amber nodded. He was quite right. She'd discovered this for herself when she'd tried speaking to some of the city Arabs.

She continued, 'Yesterday I went with a local interpreter to visit one of the Bedouin encampments near the city. I was hoping to persuade them to let me spend some time with them.' She paused and pulled a face. 'But it was a near-total waste of time. They were all terribly polite, but nobody wanted to help.'

A look of understanding flitted across Sheikh Zoltan's eyes. 'The Bedouin can be very wary of strangers. It is their way to be secretive and closed. This is what happens when people live hard and isolated lives. They become very suspicious of the world outside.'

He reached forward and took another cake from a silver platter, popped it in his mouth and chewed for a moment. Then he regarded her with a light smile. 'So, it is true what I have been told? You have been encountering a few problems getting the information you need?'

'I certainly have.' Amber leaned towards him a little, sensing a note of sympathy in his voice. 'I keep turning up for interviews that I'd set up before I even came out here and finding that they've been inexplicably cancelled. And not just at the Bedouin camp. It's been happening in town as well. It's all a bit frustrating and a terrible waste of time. And I can't afford to waste time. I've got to be back in London by the end of next week.'

'I see.' He sat back, adjusting the *kaffiyeh* over his shoulders with a flick of his elegant, olive-skinned fingers. The dark eyes held hers. 'However, I'm quite certain that a way can be found to overcome these problems. All that is required is a word in the right ear.'

'You mean you might be prepared to help? Oh, thank you! I'd really appreciate that.'

Wasn't this precisely what she'd been hoping for? Amber beamed with pleasure. And suddenly she felt even crazier than ever for that earlier mad lapse of panic.

'It will be my pleasure to help you. After all, it is important to me too that you get the information your mother requires for her book. If someone is planning to write about my country, I very much prefer that they get their facts right. So you must give Rashid a list of all the people you wish to interview and I shall see to it personally that your demands are properly met.'

'I really am grateful!' Amber spoke from the heart. 'You've no idea how much this means to me.'

'Nonsense. As I said, I'm more than happy to help you.' As he paused, an amused look fleetingly touched his eyes. 'It would never do for you leave Ras al-Houht with the impression that it is a country inhabited by disobliging and uncooperative people.' He regarded her for a moment. 'And to make absolutely certain that that is not the impression you leave with it is my intention to go even further in my efforts to assist you. . .

'Here in the palace archives I have many documents and papers that I am certain would be of considerable interest to you. Historical and social data, naturally all in English, that quite simply is not available elsewhere.' He smiled. 'I would be happy to put it at your disposal.'

Amber could scarcely believe her ears. 'I don't know how to thank you. That would be marvellous!' she breathed.

Wow! What a totally unexpected coup! She'd been planning, once she got back home to London, to spend a few days at the School of African and Oriental Studies doing a bit of additional background research, but what Sheikh Zoltan was offering her would be far more valuable.

She laughed delightedly. 'When can I start?'

'You can start whenever you like. And, since you're here, Rashid can take you to see the archives right away.'

As he spoke, he rose to his feet and clapped his hands twice. Instantly, seemingly miraculously, the bearded Rashid appeared.

Sheikh Zoltan turned to address his servant. 'Take Miss Buchanan to the archives. She will explain to you what papers and documents particularly interest her and you will kindly make them available for her to look at.'

As Rashid bowed, Amber rose from her seat to follow him, a little overwhelmed at the speed at which everything was suddenly happening. It was amazing. Just like that, all her problems had been sorted out!

But, just as she was about to leave the room behind Rashid, suddenly Sheikh Zoltan spoke.

'Oh, by the way,' he began, and there was something in his voice that caused Amber, as she turned to face him again, to feel a sudden flutter in her heart, 'now that we have come to this agreement. . . And, though he smiled, the smile was totally cancelled out by the expression that filled the piercing black eyes. A look as merciless in its harshness as the midday desert sun.

Amber held her breath and waited for him to finish the sentence, her senses jangling, already feeling threatened.

Then, as the dark eyes fixed her, she heard him inform her, 'I shall expect you to move into the palace. Right away.'

CHAPTER THREE

'MOVE IN? I'm sorry, I couldn't possibly do that!'

Amber froze in her tracks, a pulse of fear beating inside her at this totally unexpected invitation, which in truth had sounded rather more like a command.

What was going on? Why did he want her to move into the palace? And why the sudden threatening look in his eyes?

'Really, it isn't necessary. I can stay at my hotel,' she insisted.

'Nonsense!'

As Sheikh Zoltan swung round more fully to face her, Amber felt a flare of real panic in her heart. He looked like some huge, terrifying bird of prey who was about to come sweeping across the room and grab hold of her.

Well, just let him try! She held her breath and tensed, every muscle in her body getting ready to fight him off.

In fact, to her relief, he remained precisely where he was. As he looked at her, he seemed to relax his stance a bit, almost as though he'd read what she was thinking, and his tone was noticeably softer as he told her,

'It would be foolish for you to remain at your hotel. All that travelling back and forth. It would be time-wasting and inconvenient. It makes much more sense for you to move into the palace.'

He smiled, the black eyes behind the dark veils of his lashes seeming to watch her very closely. Then he continued, even more gently, his voice like warm honey,

'Naturally, it goes without saying that the decision is entirely yours...but it would give me great pleasure to offer you my hospitality—to make up for all the inconvenience and frustration you have already suffered at the hands of some of my less co-operative subjects.'

Amber was aware that some of the departed colour had begun to flow back into her cheeks. Had she panicked for nothing? Read the situation all wrong? Maybe it was just his authoritarian manner that had made his invitation sound like a command?

Maybe. But she still wasn't totally convinced.

'That's a very kind offer,' she said as he waited for her answer. 'But, if you don't mind, I'd like to think about it before I decide.'

Let's see if he'd really meant all that stuff about the decision being hers. If he tried to insist, she'd turn him down for sure.

He didn't try to insist. He simply nodded. 'Of course. Take all the time you like to think about it.' Then he smiled. 'And, talking of time...' With a quick glance at his watch, he continued, 'Perhaps I can spare a few minutes, after all. I shall accompany you and Rashid to the archives. But, first, I suggest we take a look at the library.'

He turned and said something to Rashid in Arabic. Then, with a quick, almost soundless flurry of long robes, he was leading the two of them out of the room.

The main library in the Emiri Palace was situated on the first floor and was without doubt one of the most strikingly beautiful rooms in the place.

A huge circular space with a high domed ceiling, the shelves of books arranged in a fan of concentric quarter-circles, it was a triumph of the marriage of beauty and functionality and had single-handedly made the name of the Italian architect who had designed it. Invariably, any visitors who crossed over the threshold experienced a huge thrust of pleasure and admiration at what they saw.

Amber was no exception. As Sheikh Zoltan led her through the double doors—with Rashid following a discreet couple of steps behind them—she let out a gasp of delighted astonishment and stopped in her tracks, gazing round her.

'This is marvellous!' she exclaimed. 'What a wonderful place!'

Sheikh Zoltan smiled at her praise. 'It's a fairly recent addition to the palace. It was built just over three years ago.' And she detected a note of pride in his voice as he added, 'It is one of the most extensive and most used libraries in the Arab world.'

It was at that moment that an old man suddenly appeared out of the shadows and, without waiting for permission, began to address the sheikh in Arabic. Poorly dressed, with a grey beard, he looked like some palace menial and Amber fully expected the sheikh to respond curtly to the interruption.

He did nothing of the kind. To Amber's surprise, he took the old man's arm and smiled. Then he flicked a glance across at her as he took the old man aside. 'Excuse me,' he told her, signalling to Rashid to look after her.

Rashid was at her elbow in a trice, instantly reeling off a stream of information.

'As His Highness has already told you, the library was built only a few years ago. It was one of the very first works he commissioned when he took over as emir after the death of his illustrious father. Before that, there was no library to speak of in the palace.'

He waved an expansive arm. 'And now there are more than fifty thousand books here. As you can see, His Highness sets a great deal of store on the gathering and dissemination of information. Which, of course, is why, while he was having this library built, he also had a similar one, for the use of the general public, put up in the centre of our capital city.

'His Highness,' he continued in tones of some solemnity, 'believes that education is the principal way forward for his country. And he believes also that it is the inalienable right of his people.'

'That's a very proper stance to take. I've no doubt the country and the people will benefit.'

Amber offered the required response more out of politeness than anything else, for, to be truthful, she still hadn't made up her mind about Sheikh Zoltan.

From what she'd read about him, he appeared to be a benevolent enough ruler. In the four years since his accession to the Emir throne, an impressively large chunk of the enormous oil revenue that had made his family among the richest in the Gulf had been spent on building and equipping a whole range of public amenities—schools and roads and hospitals and sports centres, as well as the magnificent library Rashid had mentioned. But to what degree these apparently responsible and generous gestures were merely an exercise in self-glorification was anyone's guess.

She flicked a glance across at him as he stood talking to the old man. On the whole, he came across as a bit of an autocrat, but she'd been rather impressed by his

treatment of the old man. There'd been a totally
unexpected spontaneous kindness in the way he'd
spoken to him and taken him by the arm.

Who was the old man? she wondered. In spite of his
appearance, could he be someone important after all,
and was that the reason the Sheikh was treating him so
considerately?

Possibly, she decided, though she was still left with
the feeling that maybe he wasn't a total tyrant.

At last, whatever business they'd had was concluded
and the old man hurried off while the Sheikh rejoined
Amber and Rashid.

'I'll just quickly show you round,' he said, sweeping
off in front of them and making Amber smile to herself
as she followed behind. This was the version she was
more familiar with!

But, though the man could at times be a little
confusing, one thing was certain: Sheikh Zoltan's library
was magnificent.

As he whisked her round on a quick tour, explaining
as he went the various categories of books and the
computerised index system, guiding her past the row of
private study cubicles, where scholars sat, heads bent,
over piles of leather-bound volumes, Amber was genu-
inely, seriously impressed. This ranked with some of the
very best libraries she'd seen. She was definitely going
to enjoy working here.

'And now, the archives. Come. Follow me.'

With another curt command, he proceeded to lead
them to a wood-panelled room strategically situated
between the main part of the library and his private
offices.

'Here in this room resides virtually the entire history

of Ras al-Houht.' He waved a hand at a row of polished mahogany drawers with shiny brass locks and gold writing in Arabic. 'In this section, for example, there are historical documents going back to the beginning of the last century.'

Another wave of the hand. 'Here we have economic reports.'

Another wave. 'Social studies.'

Yet another. 'Commerce and trade. There are copies of all documents in both Arabic and English, and, naturally, the information has also been transcribed onto computer disk.'

Pausing, he turned to look at her. 'I think you'll find much useful information here. Information that, as I said, is available nowhere else.'

He snatched a glance at his watch. 'I'm afraid I must leave you now. I shall see you later, but, in the meantime, Rashid will look after you. Just tell him if there's anything you would like to take a closer look at and I'm sure he'll be more than happy to set up the computer.'

'Oh, that would be marvellous. I'd really love that!'

Amber's brain was buzzing with excitement. This place was a positive gold-mine of information! She could feel it in her bones. She could smell it in the air.

'I wouldn't mind having a quick look at some of the historical documents, for example,' she suggested, glancing expectantly from Sheikh Zoltan to Rashid, who was already crossing to the computer and switching it on. The truth was that she would gladly have pulled up a chair and spent the rest of the day poring over the contents of these magic drawers!

The Sheikh smiled at her enthusiasm. 'You may look

at anything you wish. As I have told you, the whole lot
is at your disposal.' He started to turn away. 'But now I
must take my leave of you.' Then he paused and added,
as though it were an afterthought, 'By the way, have
you decided yet whether you want to move into the
palace?'

Amber looked at him and hesitated for only a second.
'Yes, I have,' she said. 'I think I'd like to, after all.'

That scare she'd given herself had just been silly,
she'd decided. Sheikh Zoltan was simply trying to help
her. And it was true what he'd said, that it would be
foolish to waste time travelling between the palace and
her hotel. There was so much information in the
archives for her to sift through. She wanted to use every
minute she had.

He showed no reaction at all to her decision. He
simply nodded. 'I think that's wise.'

Then he said something very quickly to Rashid in
Arabic, turned on his heel and swiftly left the room.

In the end, Amber and Rashid spent just over an hour
browsing through a variety of historical documents, and
by the time Rashid finally switched off the computer
Amber was almost dizzy with excitement.

Her instincts had been correct. This place was a gold-
mine. Her mother was going to be speechless with
delight when she saw what treasures her daughter had
stumbled on!

It was as they were heading back towards the main
library that Rashid suddenly said to her, 'His Highness
has instructed me that, after showing you the archives, I
should take you to see the room where you'll be staying
as our guest. That way, should anything not be to your

satisfaction, you can let me know at once and I shall have it put right.'

Amber smiled at him and protested, 'I'm sure the room is perfect. You really don't need to go to all that trouble.'

'It is no trouble, I assure you. And His Highness desires it.' He treated her to one of his polite little bows. 'Come. It will only take a couple of minutes.'

'Very well.'

Amber shrugged and smiled good-humouredly as he proceeded to lead her back down to the ground floor and along another seemingly endless warren of corridors. She might as well go and take a look at the room. She wasn't doing anything else, after all. And, anyway, to tell the truth, she was curious!

There was a bounce in her step as she followed the black-bearded Rashid under archways, along passageways and past half-open doorways offering tantalising glimpses of exquisite interiors, crossing the path from time to time of some hurrying, turbaned servant.

There was a whole, totally fascinating world within these walls, all just waiting to be discovered. And it was a miracle the way her luck had suddenly turned. Just wait till she told Don she'd been assigned a room at the Emiri Palace!

At last, at the end of a blue and green tiled corridor, Rashid came to a halt outside a half-open door. He pushed the door wide and stepped courteously aside.

'Please,' he invited, with another of his bows, allowing Amber to enter the room ahead of him.

Amber stepped past him into the most beautiful bedroom she'd ever seen.

What first caught her astounded eye was the gilded

four-poster bed that stood in the centre of the gold and
white tiled floor. Draped in swathes of fine white toile
and piled with delicate, laced edged pillows, it seemed
to float in the soft light that spilled from two huge table
lamps, looking rather like the barge Cleopatra must
have sailed in on her way down the Nile to meet
Antony, her lover!

The draperies of the bed were voluptuously echoed in
the swathes of satiny fabric at the tall shuttered window,
all sumptuously fringed and tasselled in gold and white.
There was a carved and gilded wardrobe. A huge white
sofa. And everywhere you looked, in virtually every
corner, stood enormous crystal vases crammed to over-
flowing with dozens and dozens of creamy-white roses,
whose sweet, wondrous perfume seemed to intoxicate
the air.

Blinking, scarcely trusting the evidence of her senses,
Amber took a deep breath and, laughing, gazed round
her. 'This is incredible!' she exclaimed, turning to
address Rashid.

Then she stopped. Rashid was gone and the bedroom
door was shut.

'Rashid!'

With a dart of panic, she rushed towards the door,
some sixth sense already warning her what she would
find.

And her instinct was correct. The door was firmly
locked.

'Rashid!'

Nothing.

'Rashid! Come back!' She wrestled with the doorhandle. Don't panic, she told herself. Any minute, he'll
reappear. This is just some mistake.

But it was an effort to keep calm and she didn't believe it was a mistake. 'Rashid!' There was a note of real anxiety in her voice now. 'For heaven's sake, somebody come and let me out!'

Nobody heard. Or, at least, nobody answered. Amber leaned against the door, fear rising in her throat, her heart beating so hard it seemed about to burst from her chest. This couldn't be happening. This had to be some kind of waking nightmare.

She beat the door with her fists. 'Let me out! Let me out!' Then with a cry of frustration, she swung round to lean against it. And that was when something over in the corner caught her eye. She straightened, feeling her heart stop dead in her chest.

What she was looking at was her suitcase, but what was it doing here? It ought to be back in her hotel room where she'd left it. As she took a step towards it, she saw that her flight bag was there too, and for a moment she just stared at them, unable to move, trying to swallow back the wave of nausea that suddenly filled her.

What was going on? She had a ghastly feeling she knew. Taking a deep breath, feeling her legs like lead beneath her, she crossed to the wardrobe and flung the gilded doors open.

Her heart slammed in her chest. She'd already guessed what she'd find, but that made the sight that met her eyes no less shocking. All her dresses and blouses and skirts and trousers were hanging in a neat row from the rail. She tore open one of the drawers. It was full of her carefully folded tops. Another drawer. All her underwear, also carefully folded. Amber stared at it all and thought she might faint.

She leaned against the wardrobe door, her brain spinning in her head. At least she didn't need to wonder what was going on any more. It was perfectly clear. Sheikh Zoltan had made her his prisoner.

This was obviously what had been on his mind from the start. She'd been lured here to the palace, the victim of an elaborate plot, and hoodwinked into believing he planned to help her with her work. Fool! Why hadn't she listened to that voice in her head that had warned her she ought to get out of this place fast? She'd allowed herself to be tempted by the bait he'd dangled before her and had ended up walking straight into his trap!

And now, here she was, locked up like a bird in a gilded cage.

It was so bizarre it was almost funny. Like something out of one of her mother's novels. She'd told herself such a thing couldn't happen, but it looked as though she'd been wrong about that.

So, now that he'd trapped her, what exactly did he plan to do with her? Her mind backtracked to their conversation out in the courtyard.

'Within the walls of this palace,' he'd been at pains to enlighten her, 'every single thing, without exception, belongs to me.'

So, was that what she was now? The Sheikh's personal possession? A piece of merchandise that he was free to do with as he pleased?

And what else was it he'd said in the course of that conversation? All too clearly, she could hear his words again, as though he were right there in the room.

'My personal philosophy regarding my possessions could be described less as the belief that they are there to receive my respect and rather more as the conviction that their purpose is to serve me. And to provide me with pleasure—whenever and however I may wish it.'

At the time, she'd felt oddly threatened by the remark and by the way his eyes had seemed to ravish her on the spot. But it had never even occurred to her that the threat might be real.

Still leaning against the wardrobe door, she closed her eyes for a moment and took a long, slow, steadying breath. She didn't want to think this. It was too outrageous even to contemplate. But though she tried to block it out the question kept pounding in her brain. Had she been brought here to the palace to become the latest recruit to Sheikh Zoltan's harem?

An image flashed across her brain of a sunken marble bath, her being led to it by a bevy of female retainers and immersed in its silky, scented waters. Lifted out again and dried with big soft towels, massaged from head to toe with sweet, precious oils, sprinkled with perfume, dressed in a long, diaphanous gown and finally escorted to the Sheikh's bedchamber. Wasn't that how this sort of thing was supposed to happen?

She struggled very hard to take the scenario no further, but, suddenly, there she was, lying on a bed of soft, silk cushions, waiting with fear in her heart for the inevitable. And now the door was bursting open and Sheikh Zoltan was sweeping through it, coming towards her in his flowing white robes, brushing aside her protests, telling her with a smile, 'Now I shall make love to you as you have never been made love to before.'

Definitely not!

Abruptly, Amber straightened. He could believe what he liked, but that was never going to be!

Tossing back her blonde hair, she marched over to

her case, threw open the lid and set it down in front of the wardrobe. Then, sending the hangers clattering, she grabbed an armful of her clothes and flung them unceremoniously into the case. No doubt he expected her just to sit here, all frail and helpless, and wait for him to come and take his pleasure. Well, he was in for a disappointment. He could go and whistle if he thought that! Belatedly, she was going to follow her own advice and get out of here just as fast as she could!

A couple of minutes later everything was packed, the case and the bag zipped shut and standing by the door. Now all she had to do was get someone to let her out, and she'd do that by creating such a terrible racket, screaming and yelling and beating the door with her fists, that it would be impossible for anyone within earshot to ignore her. Then, as soon as the door was opened, she'd be off like a shot, threatening death or dismemberment to anyone who tried to stop her.

Clenching her fists, she took a deep breath and let rip with the most ear-splitting shriek she could manage at precisely the same moment as the door flew open and Sheikh Zoltan came striding into the room.

CHAPTER FOUR

AMBER'S scream died in her throat as Sheikh Zoltan swept up to her and grabbed her firmly by the shoulders.

'What the devil's going on?' His face was like thunder. 'Have you taken leave of your senses? You'd think the place was on fire!'

Amber glared at him. 'It would serve you right if it was!' At that moment, nothing in the world would have given her more pleasure than to see his fine palace reduced to ashes at his feet. What right did he think he had to come bursting in on her like this and start pushing her around and playing the heavy?

She struggled to break free from him. 'Let go of me!' she spat. 'Get your hands off me this minute!'

All that happened was that he simply held onto her more tightly. 'What the devil were you yelling for? Have you gone mad?' he demanded to know.

'No, I haven't gone mad! Quite the opposite, as a matter of fact. What's happened is that I've finally come to my senses!'

'Well, that's not the way it sounded. I think you'd better start explaining yourself.'

As he continued to hold her, Amber told herself to stop struggling. There was no way she could break free unless he released her, and there was something deeply disturbing about this close physical battle.

His hardness against her softness. His superior power against her weakness. By fighting him she simply seemed to be inviting him to dominate her. And, though it appalled her to admit it, there was a tiny, secret part of her that actually found their struggle exciting. The whole scenario bristled with latent sexuality.

Instantly, she became still—at least, as still as she could manage, for she was so hyped up with anger that every inch of her was trembling.

'*You're* the one who'd better start explaining yourself!' she shot back at him. She didn't give a damn that he was the illustrious Sheikh Zoltan, Emir of the Princely State of Ras al-Houht. If he expected her to cave in just because of who he was, he definitely had another think coming!

Her eyes flared defiantly as she glared into his face. 'And if anyone's taken leave of his senses it's you, if you think you can get away with trying to make me your prisoner.'

'My prisoner?'

His reaction was not what she'd expected. She'd been certain that what he'd do, in his typically arrogant fashion, was point out to her that he could get away with anything he liked. Instead, rather throwing her, he actually managed to look surprised.

'My prisoner?' he echoed again. 'Where did you get a crazy idea like that?'

He was still holding on to her, though less tightly than before. Amber looked up into his face and reflected with a shiver that never in her life before had she seen such a pair of eyes. Fierce and beautiful, they burned down at her like hot coals. Look into them for too long and eyes like these would brand your soul.

Instantly, she dropped her gaze, as though to step out of the way of danger, for the power of those dark eyes, she sensed, was very real. They were capable of far more than just branding your soul. They could fill you with a helpless longing to succumb.

Carefully, she glanced up again, using her anger as a shield. 'There's nothing the least bit crazy about what I'm saying.' There was no way he was going to bluff his way out of this. 'You tried to make me your prisoner. You had me locked in my room. That's why I was yelling—for someone to come and let me out. And, believe me, I intend to start yelling again unless you release me right this minute!'

It was too much of a challenge, of course. She knew that as soon as she'd said it. So, she was not at all surprised when he failed to release her right away. She watched him as he looked down at her in silence for a moment, the dark eyes narrowed, their expression thoughtful. Then, with a frown, he stepped back and dropped his hands away.

'You're mistaken,' he said in a flat tone. 'No one locked you in your room.'

'I can assure you they did.'

Amber took a step away from him. She could still feel his fingers burning holes into her flesh, and the lingering, powerful threat of him seemed to suffocate her like a blanket.

'I'd barely stepped into the room when Rashid closed the door on me and locked it.' She paused, painfully aware of the beating pulse in her throat. 'Believe me, I'm perfectly capable of figuring out when a door is locked.'

He was watching her with a dark, shuttered look in his eyes. 'Believe me, you are mistaken. My instructions to Rashid were that he escort you to your room to see if it suited your needs. I said nothing about locking you in. That would have been most uncivil. And Rashid would never do anything unless I had ordered it.'

That was undoubtedly true. Amber opened her mouth to say so, not caring that it would be tantamount to accusing Sheikh Zoltan of lying. For he was lying. She was sure of it, though he certainly lied convincingly. But, before she could utter a word, he continued, 'I spoke to Rashid in the corridor on my way here just a moment ago. He said he'd been called away on some urgent matter concerning one of the servants and that he'd left you here, telling you he'd be back as soon as he could.'

Amber flashed him a scornful look. Did he really expect her to believe that?

'Well, I'm afraid that's not what actually happened. He simply locked the door on me and disappeared without a word!'

'Maybe you just didn't hear him, and the door was unlocked when I arrived here. In fact, there wasn't even a key in the lock.' He fixed her with a narrow look. 'As you can see for yourself, if you care to check.'

Amber frowned and slid a glance towards the open door. There certainly wasn't a key in the lock now.

But that didn't prove anything. She swivelled her eyes back to his again. 'For all I know, maybe you removed it,' she accused him.

There was a brief, jangling silence.

'I see. That is what you think?'

As he spoke, the dark eyes flashed a warning that was unambiguously echoed in the suddenly harsh tone of his voice. Sheikh Zoltan did not take kindly to accusation.

Amber was aware of a sudden nervous flare across

her skin. Perhaps she'd gone too far. He was the Sheikh, after all, accustomed to unquestioning obedience and respect, and she was a little nobody, who, in his opinion, probably, should be grovelling before him on her knees.

Pigs would fly before she'd do that, but she did lower her gaze, and amended diplomatically, in a considerably milder tone, 'All I know is that I was definitely locked in.'

'So you keep saying.'

His face was black with impatience. Amber held her breath, suddenly a little afraid of his anger. This man was all-powerful, a law unto himself. If he took it into his mind, he could crush her like an insect.

He'd been standing very still, but now, sharply, he shifted, very nearly causing her to leap back in fright as it seemed he was about to grab hold of her again. The thought of his flesh against her flesh, the power of him subduing her had sent a jolt of swift alarm, like hot fire, rushing through her.

But, to her relief, he didn't touch her. For a long moment he continued to watch her; then, in a tone stripped of emotion, carefully controlled, he put to her, 'I think the problem is that you suffer from too vivid an imagination. Though I suppose that's scarcely surprising with a novelist for a mother.'

Amber felt a plunge of relief at this sudden change of tack. 'You could be right,' she conceded, sensing it would be wise to humour him, though she didn't actually believe it was her imagination that was the problem.

Besides, if he only knew it, she was more like her father than her mother, and her father was the most down-to-earth person she'd ever known.

A Cambridge science don, Professor Douglas Buchanan was a man who, unlike his wife, whom he adored, thrived not on fantasy but on plain, hard facts. While Emily Buchanan—Amber's pretty, dark-haired mother, who could weave a story out of the most insubstantial detail—had filled her daughter's childhood with a very special kind of magic, her gentle, blue-eyed father, whom Amber physically resembled, had passed on to her his respect for demonstrable truths.

And one thing he'd taught her about such truths was that they remained truths no matter how hard one's opponents tried to prove them false. Which was why— though right now it might be a little rash to point it out—Sheikh Zoltan was simply wasting his time in his efforts to convince her that the door hadn't been locked.

It had not been her imagination. The door *had* been locked. That was the simple, unalterable truth.

But there was no point in insisting. That would only make him mad again. As a silence fell between them, Amber stared down at the floor, trying to decide what her next move should be. Before she could come to any conclusion, Sheikh Zoltan spoke again.

'So, at least, before you started yelling and shouting, I assume you had a chance to look at your room?' Amusement touched his eyes, momentarily transforming the harsh features. He raised one curious eyebrow. 'I trust it meets with your approval?'

'The room is quite beautiful. It would be very hard not to approve.'

Amber looked into his face, reluctantly intrigued by that quick, fleeting glimpse of a lighter side to his character. If it really did exist, it was buried deep, she decided, and allowed to rise to the surface only very rarely. And, at the tiniest, flimsiest provocation, it would vanish like a snowflake in the desert.

So, in spite of this brief lull, she could count on another eruption as soon as she came out with what she was planning to say next. But it had to be said. She took a deep breath and said it.

'However, I'm afraid I won't be staying after all. I've changed my mind. I don't think it would be a good idea. I've decided to go back to my hotel right away.'

Heart thumping, she waited to hear his reply. Would he try to force her to stay? What would she do if he did? One thing was sure: she'd fight him every way she could.

At least he didn't erupt instantly. He regarded her with narrowed eyes. 'Is this,' he demanded in a cool tone, 'because you believe you were locked in?'

'Yes, it is.'

She studied his expression closely. That reined-in response meant absolutely nothing. It was the deceptive quiet calm of a crouching feral cat. At any moment, when least expected, he might suddenly go for her throat.

'Don't you think,' he suggested, 'that you are, perhaps, overreacting?'

'No, I don't. I don't think I'm overreacting at all.'

Amber kept her tone firm in spite of the unnerving way he was looking at her, his intense black eyes focused on her face as though they might spirit away her will and replace it with his. She could feel herself erecting an invisible barrier to protect herself.

She continued, 'I'm afraid I'm just not happy with the situation. There's no way I'd even consider staying on now. So, if it's all the same to you, I'd like to go back to my hotel.'

This would probably mean, of course, that she'd be banned from the royal archives. More than likely, he'd also withdraw his offer to help her with her interviews. That was rather a sad blow, but it was a small price to pay to have her peace of mind restored. And, anyway, the chances were that all these generous offers had been a trick. He'd probably never really meant them in the first place.

He was watching her. 'I think you're being hasty,' he told her. 'I can assure you things are not the way you seem to believe.'

'My imagination again?' Amber's tone was openly scornful. Then she tilted her chin at him as, suddenly, she remembered something. 'I suppose I also imagined your other little surprise?' She tossed a meaningful glance at her suitcase and bag, still stood, packed and ready, by the open door. 'I suppose I also imagined finding my clothes hanging in the wardrobe?'

She fixed him with an accusing look, challenging him openly. 'Why did you do that? I'd really like to know. Why did you have my clothes and the rest of my belongings brought from the hotel without consulting me?'

'To save time. I thought you would be keen to get down to work.' A tight note of warning had crept into his voice again. It was clear he objected to his actions being questioned. 'The transfer of your things was arranged, quite simply, to relieve you of the inconvenience of having to organise the move yourself.'

'How incredibly thoughtful of you!'

Did he actually expect her to swallow that? Well, she wasn't *that* naïve, and she rather objected to his attitude. She'd every right in the world to demand an explanation—and, what's more, to express her opinion of his actions, which, looking him in the eye, she now proceeded to do.

'However, if you don't mind my saying so, it was also just a little high-handed!'

She paused, envisaging how it must have happened—his team of lackeys despatched to her hotel room to rummage about amongst her personal belongings the minute she'd agreed to move into the palace.

Or, perhaps, even before she'd agreed to move in. Perhaps before he'd even invited her to move in. It was perfectly possible that the whole thing had been arranged before she'd even set foot in the palace!

A thought occurred to her. 'And what about my bill? Don't tell me you've also dealt with that.'

He delivered her a cool look. 'Naturally,' he said.

'Well, you'd no business doing that!' Amber glared at him. 'I'm perfectly capable of paying my own bills. And I very much resent being taken over in this fashion.'

'You are too sensitive, Miss Buchanan.'

With a sharp, impatient movement that sent the fine white *kaffiyeh* fluttering restlessly round his shoulders, Sheikh Zoltan turned away, as though he'd had enough of this conversation, and went to stand by a small table on which a vase of roses stood.

'If such small things trouble you,' he put to her in a sharp tone, 'it is very plain that you have encountered remarkably few troubles in the course of your lifetime.'

'Up until now, I suppose I have. I've been lucky in that respect.'

Amber fixed him with a cool look. One thing was for sure—none of the women in his life would be able to make such a claim! Life around Sheikh Zoltan would be intolerable in the extreme!

He was watching her. 'Perhaps you are also a little too hard to please.' As he spoke, he snapped the bloom from one of the long-stemmed roses and, in a gesture that surprised her, held it to his nose to breathe its scent.

'I offer you this room—one of the most beautiful guest rooms in the palace—and in return all you can find to do is complain. I take the trouble to have your belongings transported from the hotel, in order to save you time and inconvenience, and your only reaction is to criticise your treatment. . .'

He paused and treated her to a long, scornful look. 'I fear, Miss Buchanan, that one of so ungrateful a temperament, so disposed to finding fault with everything around her, is destined to lead a life of constant dissatisfaction.' He waited a beat before adding with mocking irony, 'Clearly, you were meant for a better world than this one.'

Amber was struck dumb for a moment. She felt her cheeks flush a guilty crimson, as though it really were true that she was ungrateful and fault-finding. And she merely stared at him in stunned, half-apologetic silence as he continued, 'Such a mean, unhappy disposition in any woman would be cause for sadness, but in such a beautiful young woman it is no less than a tragedy.' As though in a subtle act of symbolism, he tossed the rose aside. 'A man's heart can only grieve at such a state of affairs.'

As Amber recovered from her shock, she almost laughed out loud. So, she was the rose with the thorn striking sadness in his heart! Sheikh Zoltan was extremely clever, but she wasn't about to fall for that!

She looked into his face. 'I'm sorry to be such a disappointment.' She actually sounded as though she meant it, but then she was quite capable of playing this game too. 'But I'm afraid,' she continued in the same earnest tone, which was a pretty close replica of the one he had used, 'that you're not the only one who's had their illusions crushed today.' She was even speaking in that slightly formal manner he always used. 'I, too, have had to bear a bitter disappointment.'

One disdainful eyebrow lifted. Curious black eyes glanced across at her. 'Oh?' he responded. 'And why might that be?'

'I accepted an invitation in good faith,' Amber enlightened him. 'An invitation to move into the palace as your guest. And I accepted it gratefully and with a great deal of pleasure. I hope you will forgive me for presuming to correct you, but I had no complaints at all at that stage.'

She paused.

He continued to watch her.

After a moment, she continued.

'My feelings only altered when I made the discovery that I was not to be your guest at all. Rather, I was to be your prisoner.'

As he seemed about to interrupt, she hurried on and informed him, 'This is indeed a beautiful room, one of the most beautiful rooms I've ever seen, and normally to stay in such a room would give me enormous pleasure. But how can one possibly find pleasure in a room, however luxurious and beautiful that room may be, when one knows that that room is in reality a prison?

'A gilded cage is still a cage, after all,' she finished eloquently.

Amber wasn't really sure what response she'd expected to this carefully reasoned and calmly delivered little soliloquy, but it definitely wasn't the one which now erupted before her eyes.

'Pig-headed woman! How many times do I have to tell you? This is all in your imagination! You were never a prisoner!' In an explosion of irritation, Sheikh Zoltan swung away. 'Come here! Let me show you something that may finally convince you!'

He headed across the floor to the shuttered window, then, as though he were tearing down a barricade, he proceeded to sweep the heavy draperies aside. As Amber came up behind him, wondering what on earth was about to happen next, he thrust open the window.

'There! Is this a prison?'

Now that the window was open, Amber could see for herself that it wasn't in fact a window at all but French doors that led out into a small courtyard shady with palms and tall pots of oleander.

Before she could say anything, however, he snatched hold of her by the wrist and, none too gently, thrust her through the open doorway, so that she hurtled out into the courtyard in a most ungainly fashion. As she pulled herself up, he gestured theatrically across the courtyard to a brown-painted arched door set in the wall.

'If you wished to escape, all you had to do was leave by that door. It is always left open and it leads out into the palace gardens.' He swung round with a scowl to face her. 'But no doubt you don't believe me. I suppose you're convinced I'm lying about this, too.'

Before she had a chance either to confirm or deny this—though she wasn't at all sure what she actually believed anyway—he was sweeping across the courtyard, his headdress flying out behind him like the banner of some warrior riding into battle. Then he snatched hold of the doorhandle and yanked the door open.

He cast a scowl like an exploding cannon across the cobblestones at her. 'There! You have your proof! Now try claiming you were a prisoner!'

Amber had watched this entire performance with a sense of total wonder. Even before he'd opened the door with such a dramatic flourish, a bit like a magician opening the door of his magic box, she'd started to sense that she actually had been wrong. She'd never been a prisoner at all.

Even if the door had been locked, she could easily have escaped. The walls of the courtyard were no more than eight or nine feet high and there were plenty of wooden benches and big clay pots to climb up on. Thanks to her weekly workouts at the local gym back home, she was pretty fit. She could have been up and over the wall in no time.

It had taken her less than a hundredth of a second to work that out. For the rest of the time all her attention had been fixed on the utterly engrossing spectacle of Sheikh Zoltan.

He was perfectly splendid in his fulminating outrage. Full of raw animal power. Wild and exciting. Every swift, masterful movement of his lean, muscular body radiated an instinctive, savage, ruthless grace.

And this power, this shimmering quality in him was not because he was a sheikh. It went far deeper than that. It was the substance, the very essence of him. It was, quite simply, the man he happened to be.

It had been impossible to tear her gaze away. Never in her life had she witnessed such an utterly awe-inspiring display of sheer, ferocious, seductive magic.

Having proved his point about the courtyard door, he was now sweeping back across the cobblestones towards her. He came to a halt in front of her and impaled her with a look.

'You have seen for yourself now, so let's have no more talk of imprisonment.' The black eyes swept impatiently over her face for a moment. 'However, the choice is yours. No one will try to stop you if you are still determined to move out of the palace. You may leave this very minute, if that is your desire. Just tell me and I shall instruct Rashid to pick up your bags and escort you without delay back to your hotel!'

Amber felt as though she'd been lifted up and carried off by a tornado. The passion and the raw energy of him quite simply took her breath away.

Earlier she'd decided that life around Sheikh Zoltan would be intolerable. At times it undoubtedly would be, but at least it would never be dull! Anything but! It would buzz with excitement. He'd breathe fire and vitality into everything he touched.

He was waiting for her response, his eyes burning into her face, and Amber was suddenly very sure what her answer should be.

'There won't be any need for Rashid to take me back to my hotel. I can see now that I was wrong and I'm sorry I accused you of making me a prisoner.'

All her earlier doubts had vanished. She'd simply misjudged him once again. The business of the locked door, of course, remained a mystery, but she was convinced now that there had to be a harmless explanation for that.

'I'd be happy to stay on here, as we originally agreed,' she assured him.

'As you wish.' His tone betrayed neither surprise nor satisfaction. He started to turn away, as though about to leave. Then he paused. 'I almost forgot. The reason I came by was to tell you that I shall desire your company at dinner tonight.' He swung off towards the door. 'I dine at nine o' clock. One of the servants will come to collect you.'

It was as she half turned to watch him go that something caught Amber's eye. A flash of snow-white behind one of the flowerpots. As she turned for a better look, her face broke into a smile.

'It's the peacock! The one I saw in the other courtyard when I first arrived.'

Sheikh Zoltan paused to glance back at her over his shoulder. 'I had him brought here,' he said. 'I thought it would please you.'

Then, leaving Amber quietly puzzling over the significance of this revelation, with a swish of his long white robes, he was gone.

CHAPTER FIVE

AMBER was seated on one of the silk brocade divans that lined the elaborately tiled walls of the dining room, a splash of light from the pierced brass ceiling-lamp bathing her head and shoulders in a gentle golden light. Sheikh Zoltan watched her and thought he had never seen a more enchanting sight in his life.

Her head was bent over a book and she was clearly totally absorbed, legs crossed at the ankles, one shapely, sandalled foot lightly tapping the air, as though in time to some private orchestra in her head. She was quite unaware that he was standing in the doorway.

He remained where he was, half-hidden in the shadows, and allowed his eyes to glide unhurriedly over her, admiring the curves of her slim, feminine figure, dressed now in a deep blue ankle-length dress, delighting in the way her cloud of blonde hair shimmered like purest spun gold in the lamplight.

As he watched, for the umpteenth time since that fateful moment yesterday, when quite by chance he had spotted her down in the Bedouin camp, he put up a prayer of heartfelt thanks for this small miracle. The more he saw her, the more he knew she was precisely what he had dreamed of but had never dared to hope might actually chance his way. And now that he had found her and drawn her into his net he must do everything in his power to make certain that she stayed.

That thought triggered a quick, anxious tug at his heart.

There must be no more locked doors. That had nearly proved disastrous and he had taken steps to ensure it never happened again. Locked doors would not be necessary. He was pretty confident of that anyway. Had he ever met a woman he could not bend to his will?

He continued to watch her. This one would be no exception. She had spirit. She might resist. But he would simply bide his time. Waiting was not a problem. He knew how to wait. Time, after all, passed slowly in the desert. And he was a son of the desert. He had patience in his blood.

As though she might have sensed his presence, all at once she glanced up and the sudden beauty of her face sent a warm rush through his heart. Zoltan smiled to himself. Right from the beginning he had known that she was the answer to his prayers, but, all the same, he had not expected to find quite so much pleasure in her.

A happy bonus indeed, he reflected with satisfaction as her gaze dropped away again, for, after all, she had not spotted him. Not only would she perfectly serve the purpose for which he required her, she would at the same time provide him with a great deal of enjoyment.

He stepped forward out of the shadows, moving soundlessly across the carpet towards her.

'Good evening,' he announced. And instantly she looked up.

'Good evening.'

Closing her book, Amber rose to her feet and he did not imagine the quick blush that touched her cheeks. Zoltan smiled to himself. No, locked doors would not be necessary. What he desired of this woman would be his for the taking.

Amber hadn't been looking forward at all to the evening. In spite of the rather charming, unexpected gesture with the peacock and in spite of the fact that she really was quite convinced that he hadn't been trying to make her his prisoner after all, she'd been afraid that dinner might prove to be an ordeal. He was so utterly unpredictable. Who knew what kind of mood he might be in?

But when he joined her in the dining room, at nine on the dot—she'd arrived a few minutes earlier with a book to keep her company, just in case he turned up late!—she knew, straight away, when at the sound of his voice she'd looked up to see him walking towards her, that she was about to be treated to a taste of his considerable charm tonight.

To her dismay, she stupidly blushed at the warm look that flowed over her. She felt an instant, quick response inside her, a sudden, foolish tightening around her heart.

Then he said, 'You're looking beautiful. As I walked through the door, it struck me that I had never seen a lovelier sight in my life.'

He was just being gallant, of course. But that was OK. At least it looked as though their dinner was going to be fairly civil. As for the gallantry...well, she'd just let it wash over her, and she'd take care to steel herself against those wickedly seductive eyes!

He led her to a low square table of beaten brass, and, touching one hand lightly to her elbow—a small, unexpected intimacy that sent a dart of awareness through her—invited her to make herself comfortable on one of the piles of coloured cushions that surrounded it.

'Naturally,' he offered, 'if you prefer, I can ask the servants to bring in a western-style table and chairs. But, since you're here to do research into the ways of my country, I assumed you would be happy to eat Arab-style.'

'Oh, I am. Perfectly happy,' Amber assured him at once, arranging her long blue dress decorously over her legs as she settled herself comfortably on the cushions. The informality of this unaccustomed style of eating rather appealed to her.

'You will now be in a position,' Sheikh Zoltan observed with a smile as he lowered himself onto the cushions opposite her, 'to describe to your mother something of the rituals of an Arab meal.'

'Just what I was thinking.' Amber smiled back at him. And as a trio of servants soundlessly appeared bearing platters of rice and mutton and *mezze* and began laying out the dishes on the gleaming tabletop she was mentally taking a note of every tiny detail. Back in her room, later, she'd write it all down.

But, as fascinating as the details of the meal itself were, what fascinated Amber most was her host.

She found herself observing him with ever increasing curiosity. Which, she kept asking herself, was the real Sheikh Zoltan? Was it the insufferable martinet she'd clashed with this afternoon or the civilised being who sat opposite her now, urging her to try a mouthful of this or that particular delicacy and entertaining her with stories of where the various dishes came from?

Probably, the truth was a mixture of the two extremes. The way he was behaving tonight—all charm and informality—seemed, to her surprise, to be totally unforced, as though it really was a genuine part of his character. But, all the same, there was no denying the seam of dark ruthlessness that lay at the back of those impossibly black eyes.

Pinning him down was a far from easy task, but at least there was one thing she was now sure of. He was not the villain she'd believed him to be earlier and she'd been mad to imagine he was planning to take her prisoner! She'd simply allowed her imagination to run riot and had ended up confusing real life with the plot of her mother's book.

'I see you enjoy Arab food,' he remarked towards the end of the evening, smiling with approval as she helped herself to a baked quince. She'd eaten everything that had been put before her, frequently coming back for seconds!

'Some Westerners,' he added, 'find it not to their taste.'

'I think Arab food is delicious.' Amber smiled back at him. 'And, anyway, I always enjoy trying new things.'

'I see. You clearly have a taste for adventure.' As he spoke, something flickered at the back of his eyes.

'I don't know about adventure. . .'

Amber dropped her gaze from his and pretended to be engrossed in peeling her quince. She'd caught that look in his eyes which had looked rather like an invitation and she'd been horrified by the answering flare inside her. Whoa! she told herself This conversation's getting dangerous.

New things. Adventure. What had seemed a harmless enough exchange was suddenly bristling with innuendo.

She picked uneasily at the quince, making a thoroughly bad job of it.

'Allow me.'

Making her jump a little, Sheikh Zoltan suddenly reached across and lifted the fruit from her fumbling fingers.

He smiled. 'Sometimes one needs a little assistance with new things.'

As he proceeded to peel it for her, Amber studiously watched his hands, not daring to raise her eyes to his face, for the brush of his fingers when he'd taken the quince from her had caused a quite ridiculous commotion in her heart. Though watching his hands as they stripped the skin from the ripe flesh was possibly even more unsettling than watching his face.

Every sure, sensuous movement of the olive-skinned fingers was sending a ripple of awareness scurrying down her spine. It was all too sinfully easy to imagine those hands working the same deft magic on her. Peeling away her dress. Caressing her naked flesh.

'There.'

At last, the quince was ready to eat. He held it out to her and smiled.

Amber still didn't dare to look into his eyes. 'Thank you,' she murmured, and reached out to take it.

But he moved it out of her reach and picked up his knife. Then he cut off a slice and held it out to her. Leaning towards her, he told her, 'Open your mouth.'

Amber hesitated, nervously flicking her eyes up to meet his and instantly wishing that she'd kept her gaze averted. The black eyes seemed to devour her, to draw her into their depths and swallow her.

'It's OK. I can manage,' she said, reaching out her

hand again. To her dismay, her voice sounded distinctly croaky.

In response, he shook his head. 'Open your mouth,' he said again.

Even if she'd actually been sure she wanted to, Amber would have been quite incapable of doing as he said. She felt quite paralysed by this intimacy. She didn't know what to do. So she just looked at him.

'What's the matter? Don't you want it?'

She swallowed. 'No, I want it.'

'Then take it.' He smiled and held the quince slice a little closer. The rapacious black eyes poured over her like molasses.

Amber still didn't make a move. She licked her dry lips. 'I can manage on my own, thanks. Really,' she said.

Sheikh Zoltan continued to watch her. 'Where's your spirit of adventure? It's obvious that no man has ever fed you a quince before, but didn't you, just a moment ago, tell me you enjoyed trying new things?'

'Yes, I did, but—'

She took a deep breath and held it, her eyes flickering anxiously from the quince to his face. He was perfectly right. No man had ever fed her a quince before. Nor an apple, nor an orange—nor anything else, for that matter! The very idea of Adrian feeding her a piece of fruit was almost enough to make her laugh out loud. Such intimate, erotic gestures definitely weren't her ex-fiancé's style. In fact, he'd probably be quite shocked if he could see what was going on now!

Despite her own currently rather tangled-up feelings, that suddenly struck her as both strange and a little sad.

'This is your last chance. If you don't eat it, I will.'

As he spoke, Sheikh Zoltan held the quince slice even

closer, so that now it was only a couple of inches from her mouth. Amber could smell its sweet perfume, but far more intense was the delicious, warm scent of Sheikh Zoltan's skin. She drank it in, excitement rising in the pit of her stomach.

And that was when she decided it was time to make a move and put an end to this seriously unwise situation. For the more she strung it out, the more she could feel the tension building. The very air seemed to crackle with sexual electricity.

She closed her eyes, held her breath and opened her mouth.

It seemed like for ever before he popped it into her mouth, and though his fingers brushed her lips for only a split second it was the longest split second she'd ever endured in her entire life. Still holding her breath, she quickly closed her mouth, tasting the clean, sharp sweetness of the fruit against her tongue, though she could almost imagine it was really the taste of his fingers.

'There. That didn't hurt, did it?'

He sat back and smiled at her, quite clearly amused by the torment she'd just come through. Sadist! But Amber was far too busy chewing and concentrating on not choking to be able to say anything. She did manage to shake her head, though, then instantly wished she hadn't, as, still smiling, he proceeded to cut another slice from the quince.

Oh, Lord! Was he going to feed her the whole wretched thing?

It seemed that he was.

He held the piece out to her, a flash of wicked humour

lighting the dark eyes. 'Don't worry. The second time's always easier.'

Amber tossed him an ironical look. 'That's a relief.'

He smiled. 'So, go on, open your mouth.'

Oh, why not? Amber smiled back at him. And opened her mouth.

He fed her the slice of fruit. 'And, after the second time, it's all downhill. By the time we're finished, you'll swear there's no other way to eat a quince.'

Maybe that was just a slight exaggeration, but by the time they were down to the last couple of slices Amber was rather enjoying his little game. That sexual electricity still buzzed between them, but it felt a lot less dangerous, more under control now that a more light-hearted note had been introduced.

She no longer felt threatened. It was just a harmless bit of flirtation. And a harmless bit of flirtation with such a powerfully attractive man was hardly the most unpleasant way of passing the time!

As a servant brought them coffee and a little dish of *halwa* and Sheikh Zoltan turned to say something to him in Arabic, Amber watched the Sheikh discreetly from under her lashes. There was a great deal more to him than she'd originally imagined and, so far, she'd barely skimmed the surface. She suspected she'd rather enjoy getting to know him better.

It was a little while later, after they'd finished their coffee, that at last he glanced at his watch and told her, 'It's nearly midnight. I think it's time I escorted you back to your room.'

Surprised, Amber glanced down quickly at her own watch. She'd had no idea it was so late. The past three hours had simply flown.

How strange, she reflected as he led her swiftly along the maze of corridors, the fine white *kaffiyeh* dancing back from his face, his long robes swishing in time to his quick strides. She'd expected the evening to be an unremitting ordeal, but, though it had had its worrying moments, it had been nothing of the kind. She'd actually enjoyed herself rather a lot.

As they reached the door of her room, Sheikh Zoltan turned to her and told her, 'I've instructed Rashid to drop by your room tomorrow morning to pick up your list of the people you want to interview. As soon as I have it in my possession, I shall get to work ironing out your problems.'

Amber smiled at him gratefully. 'That's wonderful. Thank you.' As she looked at him, she noticed how the glossy, thick black hair curled engagingly around his ears.

He was continuing, 'And, since I know you're keen to get down to work, I've made arrangements so that you can start studying the archives material tomorrow morning. I understand you've already told Rashid which files you wish to consult first.'

Amber nodded. 'Yes, I told him I'd like to start with some of the historical records.'

'Then that will be arranged. And if there's anything else you require all you have to do is speak to Rashid. He has been charged with looking after your needs.'

As he paused and looked down at her, a teasing smile touched his lips. 'I hope you are now quite happy with the situation?'

He was quoting what she'd said to him earlier after that fright with the locked door, when she'd told him she wanted to go back to her hotel, and it sounded distinctly funny to hear it now. How could she have believed all those crazy things she'd said?

Amber smiled back at him. 'I'm extremely happy with the situation.'

'Good.' He held her eyes. 'That is what I hoped to hear.' Surprising her, he reached out and lightly touched her hair. 'It would dismay me greatly if you were not happy,' he told her.

Amber did not move away. For some strange reason, the way he was touching her felt perfectly natural. Intimate but, somehow, acceptably so.

'It is important to me that my very special guest be happy,' he elaborated. 'So, if anything is not to your satisfaction, you must speak up at once.'

'Thank you. I will. But I have no complaints for now.' She smiled. 'You see, I am not so hard to please, after all.'

Their eyes met and locked. Sheikh Zoltan smiled back at her. 'That is good.' His hand still rested softly on her hair.

He's going to kiss me. The thought went spinning through her head. Amber felt herself stiffen. What would she do if he did?

The question went unanswered, for, instead of kissing her, he stepped away. 'It's late,' he said, dropping his hand from her hair. 'Time, I think, to say goodnight.'

Then, almost abruptly, he turned on his heel and walked away.

In her bed, after she'd turned out the light, Amber lay staring into the darkness for a long time. It was ages since she'd felt this way. Kind of misty and dreamy. She couldn't even remember the last time she'd spent such an enchanting evening with a man.

For it *had* been enchanting—in a silly sort of way, of course. A light-hearted, frivolous, thoroughly enchanting evening. Though, of course, there was no danger of his turning her head.

He was a hugely attractive man. She'd always been aware of that. No woman with red blood in her veins could help being attracted. He was beautiful. He was exotic. He exuded sensuality. He was exciting. He crackled with danger and romance. In short, he was the very stuff of her mother's heroines' dreams! But he was not the stuff of hers. Very definitely not. In spite of all his charm, he was a chauvinistic despot, a million miles from the sort of man who really appealed to her.

No, tonight had been enjoyable, but that was as far as it went. She found him interesting, intriguing, but she was immune to his charms. Her feet were firmly on the ground.

She turned over, drawing the light silk sheet around her shoulders. All the same, it might be wise to avoid any repetition of this evening, for she'd no desire to give him the wrong idea. He was the kind of man who wouldn't need a great deal of encouragement and she definitely didn't want any of those sorts of complications.

So, there'd be no more harmless flirting. She'd put a stop to that.

With a soft, contented sigh, she snuggled down beneath the sheet, perfectly confident in the resolution she'd just made.

In another corner of the palace, as Amber drifted off to sleep, Sheikh Zoltan was standing by his open bedroom window gazing up at the silver crescent moon.

The beautiful bird now sits happily in her gilded cage, he was thinking. Soon, it will be time to make the next move.

CHAPTER SIX

THE first thing Amber did when she awoke next morning was fling open the French window, step out into the courtyard and bid a cheerful 'Good morning!' to the peacock.

She'd slept like a top in the big four-poster bed with its scented, lace-trimmed pillows and swathes of fine white toile. How could anyone fail to sleep well in such a luxurious bed? And this morning, when she'd awakened and glanced round at the magical room, she'd smiled with a flicker of wry amusement.

'You may as well enjoy all this, Amber,' she'd told herself. 'You'll never experience anything like it again!'

As she showered and washed her hair in the gold-tiled ensuite bathroom with its huge sunken bath and shelves stacked high with jars filled with soaps and bath gels in every fragrance known to woman—Amber had chosen one that smelled deliciously of jasmine—she decided that the very first thing she would do was sit down and write out that list for Rashid.

She must also be sure to tell him she'd need the use of a fax machine, for now that she'd as good as sorted out all her problems she ought to get in touch with Don in London at once and tell him to go ahead with his planned trip to California. She'd be back in the office to cover for him at the end of next week, as promised.

Then, after she'd spoken to Rashid, she'd head straight for the library, hopefully tracking down some-where to have breakfast on the way, for in spite of last night's far from modest dinner she was aware of the occasional sharp pang of hunger. At the very least, a cup of coffee and a slice of toast were called for.

It was as though someone had read her thoughts. As she emerged from the bathroom, rubbing herself dry on a huge soft white towel that smelt as though it had been washed in rose petals, there was a tap on the door and a voice announced, 'Breakfast!'

'Just a minute!'

Amber darted back into the bathroom and grabbed the robe that hung on a peg behind the door. As she hurriedly pulled it on and, a trifle breathlessly, re-emerged, the bedroom door opened and in walked a servant carrying a tray laden with croissants and almond pastries and filling the air with the delicious aroma of fresh coffee.

'Good morning, miss,' he greeted her, in halting English with a broad smile.

It was the same servant who'd escorted her to the dining room yesterday evening. A bright-looking boy of eighteen, his name was Tariq.

Amber smiled back at him, pleased to see him again. 'Good morning, Tariq. Just put the tray down there,' she began, indicating one of the coffee-tables that were scattered about the room.

But perhaps he hadn't understood, for, totally ignoring her instructions, he crossed to the French doors and stepped out into the little courtyard.

Amber followed him, smiling. This was a much better idea! Why hadn't *she* thought of having breakfast al fresco? But then she frowned as she saw, beneath one of the palm trees, a rectangular wooden table and a couple of wooden chairs that definitely hadn't been there less than fifteen minutes ago. How odd. Someone must have brought them while she was having her shower.

Oh, well. She shrugged to herself. Strange things kept happening in this place. She might as well just start getting used to it!

As Tariq laid out her breakfast, she looked out a notepad and pencil. While she was eating, she'd quickly write out Rashid's list. Then, as Tariq disappeared, she sat down at the table, poured herself some coffee and helped herself to a sticky pastry, noticing that the peacock was having breakfast too, for someone had brought him a bowl of fruit and nuts.

'*Bon appetit!*' she told him, and took a mouthful of her coffee.

She was just finishing off her list and her third almond pastry—she'd have to go on a diet at this rate once she got home!—when the little wooden door at the end of the courtyard opened and in walked two men, each carrying a large cardboard box.

Greeting her with a nod, they came up to where she was sitting and laid the two boxes on the ground beside her. Then, without uttering a word, they turned and walked away again.

Amber had managed with great difficulty to keep a straight face throughout this performance. She'd been absolutely right. Strange things definitely kept happening! Curious, she bent down and peered inside the boxes, one of which was filled with various kinds of stationery, the other with a selection of leather-bound files. She pulled out one of the files and peered at it more closely.

It was one of the archive files that she'd told Rashid

she wanted to work on. But why had it been brought here? There must be some mistake. Maybe these men didn't know she was planning to work in the library.

She jumped to her feet. 'Wait a minute! Hang on!' But they were already disappearing back out through the wooden door. As she started to hurry after them, the door clicked shut—or had that been the sound of a key turning in the lock? Before she could go and check, a voice behind her spoke, almost making her jump out of her skin.

'They've gone, I'm afraid, and they don't understand English anyway. Whatever your problem is, you'd better tell me.'

Amber whirled round, instantly recognising that voice, and found herself looking into Sheikh Zoltan's dark-eyed face.

'What's up?' he demanded. 'Is there something wrong?'

'Yes, I think there might be.'

Amber was catching her breath, still reeling from the way her blood had rushed at the sight of him. For it had. She'd been totally unable to control the almost violent physical reaction when she'd looked into his face. It had felt like an electric current jolting through her.

'So, tell me. . .what seems to be the matter?'

He was standing beside the open French window, its arch providing a dark, dramatic frame for his tall, imposing, white-clad figure. Very still, he was watching her with strangely shuttered eyes.

And perhaps it was that closed look combined with the anger she felt at herself for having reacted to the sight of him in that ridiculously inappropriate manner that caused a sudden suspicion to leap into her head.

The files hadn't been brought here by mistake, after all. Something else was going on and she sensed she knew what it was.

She waved towards the two boxes. 'I'm a little confused,' she began. Play this cool, she was telling herself. Don't start accusing him of anything. There's just a chance you could be wrong, after all. 'I can't understand why all this stuff's been brought here.'

'For your convenience, of course. According to Rashid, these are the files you said you wished to begin by studying. The other box contains a selection of stationery for your use.'

'But why have they been brought here? That's what I'm asking. They're no use to me here if I'm going to be working in the library.'

He paused for just a millisecond before answering. When he spoke, there was a flat edge of warning to his tone.

'I agree, but you're not going to be working in the library.' He fixed her with a dark look. 'You're going to be working here.'

'That was not what I'd understood.' So, her suspicion *had* been right. Rebellious anger flared inside her. 'It was my understanding that I'd be working in the library.'

'Then you misunderstood. That was never on the agenda.'

'May I ask why?'

'You will be more comfortable here.'

'More comfortable? What exactly do you mean by that?'

He still hadn't moved from his position by the window, but he gestured now towards the table beneath the palm tree. 'As you can see, I have had a table installed for you to work at. You will be extremely private here. No one will disturb you. And Rashid is only a phone call away. From the phone in your room, you may call him for anything you need.'

'I appreciate that. And I really am most grateful.'

Amber bit back her frustration and forced a diplomatic smile. If she wasn't careful, he'd start accusing her of being ungrateful and hard to please again and she could do without a repetition of that!

'However,' she continued, 'I'd be equally comfortable in the library. And, if you don't mind, I'd actually prefer it.'

'That is unfortunate.'

With a quick, impatient movement, he stepped away from the window, causing the white *kaffiyeh* to flutter back from his face, revealing the proud, sculpted lines of his profile. He came to stand a couple of feet away from the snow-white peacock, which was pecking at some fruit seeds that had spilled to the ground, and it occurred to Amber that they bore a striking resemblance to one another.

The perfect snowy whiteness in which they were both clothed. The proud, haughty bearing. The aristocratic gaze. Though, of the two, by far the more beautiful was Sheikh Zoltan.

Instantly, she crushed that thought, angry that she'd even thought it, and watched as he turned to face her again and continued, 'It is unfortunate because I'm afraid it cannot be. You will do your research here. That is the arrangement.'

'And what if I don't like it? What if I don't want to do my research here?' She paused and fixed him with an angry, accusing look. 'What if I don't want to be treated like a prisoner?'

'So we are back to that again?' He let out an irritated breath. 'How can you be a prisoner when none of the doors are locked? You are not a prisoner. You are perfectly free.'

'Am I? Well, if I'm so free, why can't I work in the library?'

The black eyes flashed her a warning. In a tight tone, he told her, 'Because, I'm afraid, it would not be convenient.'

Amber flashed a defiant look back at him. 'Not convenient for whom? I can assure you it would be perfectly convenient for me.'

'That may be. However, there are other considerations.'

He paused and breathed slowly, as though carefully reining in his anger. When he continued, his voice was low and controlled.

'Your presence would not be convenient for the other users of the library.'

'Not convenient in what sense?'

'In the sense that it would be distracting.'

'Distracting?' Amber frowned and then suddenly she understood. 'Are you telling me I'm not allowed to work in the library because I'm a woman?'

Black eyes narrowing, he looked straight at her. 'Yes, that is what I'm telling you. This isn't England, you see. Our customs are different. Here, the sexes do not mix freely.' There was no hint whatsoever of apology in his tone. 'And for that reason I'm afraid you may not use the library.'

His tone was flat and firm and final.

'I see.' Two short syllables, but they fairly bristled
with condemnation. Amber fixed him with a look of
dark disapproval, aware that two totally conflicting
reactions were battling inside her at that moment.

She was sorry he'd turned out to be just another
shameless champion of the systematic oppression of
women, yet at the same time, for more immediate
personal reasons, she was glad. The resolution she'd
made to keep him firmly at arm's length would now be
that much easier to uphold, for there was no way she
could ever be seriously attracted to such a man.

He was continuing, 'I suspect you were already aware
of our customs before you came here. If you were not
prepared to accept the rules, then you should not have
come. But now that you are here I really would suggest
that it is only good manners for you to comply with our
rules.'

Fair enough. Amber had no argument with that.
She'd always believed that if you chose to go to a
country it was only right that you respected its customs.

But that didn't mean you had to approve.

In a cutting tone, she told him, 'I think such customs
are a disgrace—but, yes, I suppose I have no choice but
to accept them. And to accept the arrangement that I
work in my room.'

'In the courtyard,' Sheikh Zoltan corrected her.
'There is no need for you to feel closed in. That is why I
had the table set up out here. At this time of the year, it
is pleasant to be out of doors. Far more pleasant, I can
assure you, than being cooped up in the library.'

As he spoke, he treated her to one of those rare
smiles that so entirely transformed his face, and allowed

his dark gaze to flow over her for a moment. Warm and sensuous. As intimate as a caress.

Amber did not smile back. She simply scowled at him more fiercely, though her senses had flared in response to that look.

'And, of course, as I have already told you,' he continued, quite unmoved by her black look, perhaps even a little amused by it, 'anything you require, you just have to let Rashid know and he will see to it at once.'

Amber continued to glare at him. 'I'll need a fax machine. Immediately.' How she wished she could smack that amused look from his face.

But it continued to hover. 'I'm sure that can be arranged. I expect you need it,' he enquired, 'to keep in touch with your mother?'

'I may well contact my mother if I need to clarify anything with her.' Her eyes told him this was really none of his business. 'But, more urgently, I need to get a fax off to Don to let him know what's going on.'

'Don?' One curved coal-back eyebrow lifted. 'Who is Don? A boyfriend, perhaps?'

'No, he's not, as a matter of fact. Don's my business partner.'

'I see.' Sheikh Zoltan nodded. He regarded her curiously. 'And is there a boyfriend? I'm sure there must be. A girl as beautiful as you must have many boyfriends, I am certain.'

Amber fixed him with a cool look. 'I have several male friends.' It had never been her style to have 'many boyfriends'. By nature she was strictly monogamous.

Unlike you, she thought now, glaring into his face and suddenly recalling her initial assumption that he would, without doubt, have a whole harem of wives—a small detail, she reflected, irritated at herself, that had somehow completely slipped her mind last night when she'd been responding like some simple-minded idiot to his flirtations.

He continued to watch her curiously. 'So there's no one special in your life?'

'No, not at the moment.' There'd been no one at all since she'd broken up with Adrian.

'I thought not.' He smiled. 'After all, you don't wear a ring.'

'I don't believe in rings.'

That seemed to amuse him. 'I was not aware,' he observed, 'that such a woman existed.'

'Well, now you know she does.'

Amber glared right through his smile. It wasn't entirely accurate to say she didn't believe in rings, for she had a couple of simple rings she sometimes liked to wear, but the point was that Sheikh Zoltan had got her meaning. She didn't believe in rings as displays of wealth or status. Engagement rings and wedding rings. Rings bristling with diamonds. These were the types of rings she didn't believe in. She found herself adding, without thinking what she was saying, 'Even when I was engaged, I never wore a ring.'

A look of interest crossed his face, making Amber instantly curse herself. What had possessed her to say a stupid thing like that? Her brief engagement and the traumatic ending of it six months ago were the very last subjects she felt like getting onto.

But now it looked as though she wasn't going to have much choice.

'So, you were engaged to be married?' Sheikh Zoltan

was openly inquisitive. 'What happened? Why did the marriage not take place?'

Amber gritted her teeth. 'Because I broke off the engagement.'

'I see.' The black eyes studied her face for a moment. 'And what caused you to break off the engagement?' he asked.

This was all too familiar territory. How many times over recent months had she been asked by her family and friends to explain herself? And how desperately she hated it. It made her feel so defensive. If only she could answer, Because he was unfaithful. Or, Because he drank or, Because he beat me. But none of these was true. Adrian had been a model prospective husband. She'd broken off the engagement because of a sudden fear within her that, if she went ahead with the marriage, she'd be making a terrible mistake.

It had suddenly felt all wrong. Without really knowing why, all at once in her heart she'd been very certain that she simply couldn't marry this man everyone said was so right for her.

All this went rushing through her head as she opened her mouth to reply, but there was no way she was about to bare her soul to Sheikh Zoltan.

In a curt tone, she told him, 'I'm afraid I changed my mind.'

'Just like that?'

'Just like that.'

Her heart was beating inside her. That made her sound callous and she hadn't been callous. She'd suffered as much as Adrian during that ghastly time.

Sheikh Zoltan subjected her to a long look. 'Perhaps,'

he suggested, 'you already knew you would change your mind when you decided not to accept his ring.'

The implication of that stung and it was miles from the truth anyway.

'There was no ring to accept,' Amber informed him coldly. 'I already told you I don't believe in rings.'

'So you did.' He smiled a small, cynical smile. 'And, as I told you, I find that most unusual. I have never met a woman who does not believe in rings. Women here believe very firmly in rings. In fact, they believe very firmly in every kind of jewellery.'

'I expect they do.' Amber tossed him a scathing look. 'No doubt they consider it as some kind of compensation. Something to make up for not being allowed to use the library.'

She paused and added, her tone tight and cutting, 'Personally, I'd rather have my freedom than all the jewellery in the world.'

A tingling silence fell.

The black eyes held hers fast.

I've got to him, Amber thought. He didn't like that one bit. She felt a dart of satisfaction at this small victory and added, 'I expect all your wives are literally dripping with jewellery. They, even more than most, I imagine, must feel the need for compensation.'

To her annoyance, he smiled. 'Perhaps you could be right. That is, of course, if I had any wives.'

'You mean you're not married?'

'Only to my work.'

Amber looked at him, not at all certain if she believed him. But, before she could say anything, he was turning to go, observing over his shoulder as he went, 'Talking about work, it's time I left you to get on with yours and time I got on with some of my own.' At the French doors, he paused. 'I shall speak to Rashid about the fax machine and ask him to install one for you immediately.'

With that, he swept through the doorway and was gone.

Amber stood staring after him, but she wasn't thinking about the fax. What was actually on her mind, she suddenly realised, was what he'd just told her a moment ago. Could it really be true that, after all, he wasn't married?

What the devil is it to you? Impatiently, she turned away, heading for the table under the palm tree. He's the last man in the world whose marital status should concern you. A bullying, chauvinistic, despicable tyrant. The only thing you should be worrying about is steering well clear of him.

And it was probably a lie anyway. Everything he'd ever told her was probably a lie. She'd be mad to trust a single word he said. Such as his assurance that the doors weren't locked, for example—which instantly reminded her of that ominous click she'd heard when the servants had left. Abruptly she changed direction and strode towards the wooden door. Let's just see if it really was unlocked, after all!

At first, it seemed that it wasn't. There was a momentary resistance as Amber twisted the handle and pushed. But the following instant the door burst open and, as she catapulted out into the garden, Amber very nearly collided with what had been causing the obstruction.

A woman, heavily veiled and dressed from head to toe in black.

It was the first woman she'd set eyes on since she'd

come to the palace. She smiled at her, about to introduce herself and say hello. But with a little anxious cry the woman turned to flee.

'Wait! It's all right! Come back!' Amber called after her.

But she might have saved her breath, for the woman had gone.

CHAPTER SEVEN

IN SPITE of her initial protests, Amber had to concede that working out in the courtyard suited her very well. It was quiet and private and, as Sheikh Zoltan had also observed, at this time of year it was pleasant to be out of doors.

In a couple of months' time, of course, that would no longer be the case. Then, as the temperature started soaring into the nineties and beyond, the only comfortable place to be would be the air-conditioned indoors. But, for now, the temperature was hovering around the mid-seventies. Rather similar to a typical English summer.

She spent the entire morning engrossed in one of the files, reading about the history of Ras al-Houht—in particular, about the ancient pearl fishing industry that, before the discovery of oil just over three decades ago, had provided its people with their meagre livelihood.

Just after one o'clock, Tariq appeared with her lunch—a delicious chicken salad and a mango sorbet. Amber ate at the table outside, still poring over her file, for she was so totally absorbed that she couldn't put it down. Ras al-Houht, in spite of its odious ruler, just had to be one of the most fascinating places on earth.

It was as she was coming to the end of the file and enjoying the last mouthful of her mango sorbet that, suddenly, she had the feeling that someone was watching her. She glanced across at the door, wondering if

Tariq had come back for her lunch tray. But the doorway was empty. There was nobody there.

Then something made her glance up and, for the first time, she noticed a small half-shuttered window set high above the open French window. As she squinted at it, she was almost certain she saw a dark shadow move away. And, though she couldn't see clearly, some instinct told her that it was the woman she'd surprised earlier at the courtyard door.

How strange. Who could she be? And why was she watching her? Curious, she peered at the window for a moment longer. Then she dropped her gaze away. There was no one there now.

Leaning back in her chair, she sighed and stretched her cramped muscles. I need a break from all this reading, she decided, pushing aside the file. Suddenly, what she really fancied was a nice refreshing shower.

It was exactly what she'd needed. Twenty minutes later, she emerged from the bathroom feeling a great deal better. Pulling her robe around her, she crossed to the wardrobe. She'd just slip on a fresh dress and get back down to work. But at that moment she heard the bedroom door open behind her.

Amber turned round, expecting to see Tariq. She must have somehow failed to hear his customary polite tap. But it wasn't Tariq. She found herself looking at Sheikh Zoltan.

She glared at him. 'I didn't hear you knock,' she accused him. As she spoke, she snatched her robe more tightly around her, though she was already perfectly decent as it was.

'I suspect that was probably because I didn't knock.'

He fixed her with an amused look, quite clearly understanding that she'd already worked that out for herself.

'Really? Well, where I come from no man with any manners would ever dream of walking into a lady's bedroom without knocking!' She knew that sounded pompous, but she was so spitting mad that she didn't care.

He came sweeping right up to her. 'Is that so?' he purred contemptuously. 'But you are not at home now. Here different rules apply. In this part of the world, the observance of good manners is not generally what is uppermost in a man's mind when he walks into a woman's bedroom.'

His eyes flashed as they held hers. 'And I can assure you it is not what is uppermost in mine now.'

'That's perfectly obvious!'

Amber blazed a look back at him, but she was having to fight to hang onto her anger. All sorts of other bizarre emotions were getting in the way.

As she stood there facing him, clutching the neck of her robe, burningly aware of the fact that she was wearing nothing underneath and of the even more troubling fact that he was aware of it too, she could feel the sharp, sweet tremor of excitement in her heart. The overwhelming, raw electricity of his nearness.

Her eyes kept drifting to his mouth, imagining how it might feel against her own. At the thought, she held her breath, desire twisting in her loins.

She was appalled at herself. It was quite clear she was going mad. He'd just walked into her room with heaven knew what on his mind and she was a whisker away from inviting him to go ahead!

Marshalling what little sanity she still seemed to be in

possession of, she tilted her chin at him and demanded, 'So, perhaps you wouldn't mind explaining exactly what *has* brought you barging in here.'

She swallowed, scarcely daring to imagine what he was about to answer.

Sheikh Zoltan said nothing for a moment or two. He simply stood there, his gaze straying over her flushed face, the look in his eyes rather plainly suggesting that it would please him to convert her anger to a different kind of passion. If he tries to make a pass, I'll make him sorry, Amber promised herself, clenching her fists and pushing back her shoulders, as though to lend strength to her dangerously precarious will.

At last, he spoke.

'I came to tell you something. I have some news for you that I'm sure will greatly interest you. It concerns these interviews you were so keen to arrange.'

'The interviews?' Instantly, Amber forgot everything else. She raised expectant eyebrows. 'You mean you've managed to arrange them?'

'Naturally.' He held her eyes. 'Didn't I say I would? And, once I give my word, I always keep it,' he assured her. 'I never make promises that I do not intend to keep.'

Amber wondered why she found that statement faintly threatening. Had he made any other promises she ought to know about? She was aware of a quick, skittering shiver down her spine.

She told him, 'I never doubted that you'd do as you said.' And it was only as she said it that she realised it was true. It hadn't even crossed her mind that he might let her down.

Naturally, she knew he had the power to help her. A

snap of his elegant, autocratic fingers was all that would
be needed to get his uncooperative subjects to toe the
line. But someone else in his position might have chosen
not to bother. Somehow she'd known that wouldn't be
his way.

'I'm just surprised you managed to do it so quickly,'
she told him. Rashid had warned her, when he'd come
to collect her list and install the fax machine, that she
shouldn't expect to hear anything until tomorrow.

Sheikh Zoltan smiled at her. 'It was not difficult to
arrange. A couple of phone calls, as I said.' He watched
her for a moment. 'Rashid has the details and I have
given him instructions to pass them on to you. But the
interviews have been arranged over the next five or six
days, two or three a day, with the first couple tomorrow.
I trust that this arrangement meets with your approval?'

'It sounds perfect. I'm really grateful. But what about
the trip to the Bedouin camp?'

'That, too, has been arranged.' A light smile touched
his eyes. 'You are to go to the Wadi Ayva camp up in
the north of the country. It is quite a distance away. A
couple of hours' drive. But you will find it far more
interesting than that other camp you visited. It is far
more authentic. It is in the real desert, not the tourist
desert. And besides—' he smiled '—the headman is a
relative of mine.'

'Really?'

Amber was surprised—though she wasn't sure what
surprised her. Was it the fact that this great sheikh had
such lowly relatives, or the fact that he'd so readily
admitted it?

He seemed to read her mind.

'We are all Bedouin under the skin.' There was pride

in his voice as he went on to elaborate, 'My ancestors, for many hundreds of years, were nomads. The al-Khalifas have lived in tents for far longer than they have lived in palaces.'

At the look on her face, he smiled and added, 'It is important that a man should not forget his roots.' He raised one dark eyebrow. 'Do you not agree?'

'Oh, I agree absolutely.'

Amber said it with feeling. She'd always been fascinated by her own family history and particularly by the tales her father would tell her about his grandfather, who'd been a humble Highland crofter.

'It's all part of knowing who you are,' she added. 'The lives our ancestors led are a part of us too.'

She believed that strongly, though she knew that lots of people didn't. Some even considered it a rather strange notion. Adrian, for example, used to tease her about it. But she could tell that Sheikh Zoltan both understood and shared her feelings. That surprised her. She'd assumed they wouldn't share any beliefs at all.

He smiled at her and seemed to read her thoughts again. 'So we've finally found something we're able to agree upon.'

Amber didn't smile back. She felt suddenly uneasy and acutely conscious again of her state of semi-undress. It was as though, all of a sudden, a barrier had been broken down, and she preferred to have her barriers firmly in place.

Quickly, she changed the subject. 'This trip to the camp. . . If you remember, I mentioned I'd like to spend some time amongst the Bedouin. Will that be possible at Wadi Ayva?'

'It will. I've arranged for you to spend a couple of

days there. In that time you should be able to observe a great deal, and you will be free to take photographs and speak with whomever you wish.

'I would warn you, however, that if you have any phone calls to make you must make them before you go to the camp. There are no phones there and, naturally, no faxes.'

'I'll remember that. Thanks.' Amber was smiling to herself. What he'd fixed up was exactly what she'd been hoping for. 'I'm really grateful,' she told him. 'You've been incredibly helpful.'

'It is my pleasure to help you.' He smiled as though he meant it. Then he continued, 'I have put Rashid at your disposal. He will act as interpreter and escort you by car to the various interviews. That will be much more convenient for you than having to rely on taxis.'

'Thank you.'

She kept it to herself, but privately she was wondering if the real reason why Rashid had been enlisted to escort her was that Sheikh Zoltan didn't approve of women travelling around on their own in taxis. Last time he'd pretended to be doing something for her convenience— when he'd insisted that she do her research in her own quarters—it had really been because he didn't allow women to use his library!

She was instantly rather glad that negative thought had occurred to her. It might serve to neutralise some of the rather too positive ones she'd been having!

But, whatever his true reason might be, it didn't matter in the slightest. The arrangement couldn't have been more perfect. In between going off to do her interviews she'd be able to get on with her research and have everything wound up before the end of next week, as planned.

She felt a great warm tide of relief rush through her at the thought of this happily imminent conclusion. Staying at the palace as the privileged guest of the Sheikh amidst all this unbelievable luxury ought to have been a wonderful experience. And, undoubtedly, it would have been if it hadn't been for Sheikh Zoltan. But whenever she was around him she felt vulnerable and on edge. In spite of what she thought of him, she felt helplessly drawn, and that element of helplessness made her anxious and uncomfortable.

She simply wasn't able to control the feelings he aroused in her, and, though she'd told herself she could resist him, frankly now she wondered. Sometimes when she looked at him she seemed to have no resistance at all.

But now release was in sight. A week from now she'd be gone and, in the meantime, their paths were unlikely to cross much. She'd be spending most of her time in the courtyard with her files or out on interviews with Rashid. Then, for a couple of days, she'd be away at the Bedouin camp, where he wouldn't even be able to get in touch with her by phone!

She breathed a grateful sigh. Surely, with a little care, she ought to manage to stay out of his clutches?

'So, everything is in order now. That is good. I am pleased.' Sheikh Zoltan turned away and moved across the room, widening the distance between them, allowing Amber to relax a little.

He glanced about him. 'Ah. I see the fax machine has been installed. I trust you have managed to send off that fax you were so anxious about?'

Amber was watching him, thinking that he looked like some prowling desert cat. Smooth and sleek. Danger on silent paws.

'Yes, I have,' she told him. 'I did that straight away.'

'Good.' As he looked at her, unexpectedly he smiled. 'So, while I am here, is there anything else that you require?'

Had it not been for that smile, Amber would simply have said no. But, to her annoyance, his smile had sparked a warm response inside her. She'd felt a flurry in her heart, a quick flare in her loins.

She looked at him, suddenly determined to create a note of discord between them. 'Actually,' she said, 'it's not a request. . .but there is one small thing I'd like to mention.'

'Oh?' Black eyebrows lifted. 'And what might that be?'

'I seem to be being followed. Or spied on or something.' She paused. 'There's this woman. . . She seems to be terribly interested in me for some reason.'

'Woman?' The black brows drew together in a frown. 'What woman is this? What do you mean she's been spying on you?'

'She was outside the courtyard door this morning. When I opened the door, I almost bumped into her. I tried to speak to her, but she ran away.'

Amber had half expected that he'd just brush her story aside and tell her she'd been imagining things again, but instead he'd listened with careful attention, the beginnings of a dark scowl shadowing his face.

'Is this all?' he enquired. 'Just one incident this morning?' There was a harsh edge to his tone that hadn't been there before.

How interesting. Amber watched him curiously now as she answered.

'As a matter of fact, it's not. Just a short while ago, while I was sitting reading out in the courtyard, I was suddenly aware of someone watching me. When I looked up at the window above the French doors I'm pretty certain I saw the same woman again. I didn't get a good look because she was in shadow and, anyway, she disappeared almost immediately.'

'I see.' A look of frank displeasure crossed his face. 'And you definitely think it was the same woman as before?'

'Like I said, I can't be sure. But, yes, I think it was.' Amber was really curious now, for she could tell he knew who the mystery woman was. 'Who is she?' she came straight out and asked him.

He hesitated for just a second. Then, abruptly, he turned away. 'No one of any importance. No one you need to know about.' A dark glance over his shoulder forbade her to ask more, but that just made her all the more determined to have an answer.

'Why don't you want to tell me?'

'The woman's identity does not concern you. I shall see to it that she stops bothering you immediately. And now I suggest we drop the subject.'

But Amber refused to be fobbed off. 'Is she a servant?' she persisted.

A shutter had dropped across his eyes. He half turned to look at her. 'Yes, if you like,' he agreed. 'She is a servant.'

Amber didn't believe him. He'd only said that to shut her up. Besides, hadn't every servant she'd encountered so far been male? No, that woman is definitely not a servant, she decided.

So, who was she? And why was he so angry that she'd been spying on her? And why had the woman been spying on her, anyway?

But it was clear she wasn't about to get any answers from him now. He was turning away, heading for the door. 'I think it's time,' he was saying, 'that I left you to get dressed.' The conversation was being terminated whether she liked it or not.

Amber didn't insist. It would only be a waste of time. But there was one thing she did want to know before he left.

She called after him just as he was about to lay his hand on the door handle. 'This trip to the Bedouin camp. . . When has it been arranged for? I'd like to do a bit of research before I go.'

Sheikh Zoltan paused to look back at her. 'It will be in a couple of days' time.' He waited a beat, then observed, watching her closely, 'Naturally, you will understand that it would not be considered proper for you to make this visit to the camp unaccompanied. As we have already discussed, this is Arabia not England.'

'Of course. I understand that.' No doubt Rashid would be accompanying her. But she'd no objection to that. She rather liked the man.

She smiled. 'I hope Rashid doesn't mind being monopolised by me like this?'

He had half turned away again, about to pull open the door, but now he swivelled round to look at her once more. And a split second before he spoke, Amber knew what he was about to say. She looked into his face with a shiver of horror as he told her, 'I'm afraid Rashid will not be accompanying you to the Bedouin camp. For those two particular days your companion will be me.'

He smiled. 'It will be a chance for us to get to know each other better. For my own part, I am looking forward to it immensely.'

Then as Amber stood there, struck dumb, he swept out the door.

CHAPTER EIGHT

'Isn't she beautiful? Didn't I promise I would find her for you?'

Zoltan smiled as he looked into the velvet dark eyes of the little girl who knelt on the window-seat beside him. And deep in his heart he felt a huge tug of relief at the wonderful sparkle that lit up those eyes. It was a sparkle that for far too long had been missing, but miraculously, since Amber's arrival, it had returned.

The child, who was five years old, though small for her age, had turned to look at him, a curious frown on her face. 'Where did she come from, *abba*?' she wanted to know. 'Is she an angel sent from heaven?'

'Perhaps, in a way. I suppose you could say that.' As the little girl turned to look out the window again, Zoltan did likewise, his gaze following the child's. 'Most certainly, I have never seen anyone who looks more like an angel.'

He was sitting on the window-seat that overlooked the little courtyard where Amber was seated at her table beneath the palm tree, head bent as she pored over the file that lay open before her. She was wearing a lilac-blue kaftan that looked quite stunning with her blonde hair and the soft rosy gold of her lightly tanned skin.

Zoltan studied her with close attention, as one might study a beautiful painting. Yes, he was thinking, she really does look like an angel.

'You won't let her go away?' The child had turned again to look at him, a worried look shadowing her dark eyes. 'I don't want her to go away. I want her to stay.'

'Don't worry, *habibiti*. She won't go away.'

'And will I get to meet her soon, as you promised?'

'Of course, *habibiti*. A promise is a promise.'

Gently, he leaned towards her and laid a reassuring hand round the small shoulders, his eyes full of love and concern as he looked down at her.

'Don't worry,' he said again, bending quickly to kiss the top of her dark head. 'You'll get to meet your angel soon and she won't go away. I promise you you have nothing to fear.'

As the child leaned against him, her worried look dissolving, he watched her for a moment, wondering as he often did at the power of love she ignited in his soul. There was nothing he would not do for her, to keep her safe, to ensure her happiness. Nothing and no one mattered more to him in the whole world.

At that moment, in the doorway of the room in which they sat, a woman appeared, dressed from head to toe in black.

As she addressed Zoltan, her eyes were respectfully downcast, but an observer would have noted that the carefully averted features were not the features of the older woman she at first appeared to be. Her skin was smooth and unlined. She was probably no more than twenty-eight or twenty-nine.

She said, 'I've come to take Maha. It's time for her nap.'

Hearing the woman's voice, the child swivelled round with a cry of pleasure. '*Ummi!*' she cried, a smile lighting up her face. Then, turning quickly to embrace

Zoltan first, she slid from the window-seat and ran to the woman who was holding out her arms to her.

'My beautiful little girl!' she cried, scooping the child up and kissing her.

Zoltan watched the scene with an indulgent look, though his eyes, as he smiled, were fixed only on the child. As his gaze flicked to the woman, his eyes darkened with displeasure.

'Make sure you stay with her,' he said. His tone was as rough as sandpaper. 'Don't leave your quarters. Remember what I warned you. Next time you disobey me you'll be in serious trouble.'

By way of a response, the woman nodded soundlessly, turning away as she did so to hide the rebellious spark in her eyes. Then as Zoltan waved her away dismissively she headed towards the door, still carrying the little girl in her arms.

'I'll see you later, *habibiti*! Have a nice nap.'

As he called after the child, Zoltan's tone was warm again, and the child responded by turning with a smile and blowing him a kiss.

For a long moment after they'd gone, Zoltan continued to stare at the door, dark brows frowning, a myriad thoughts going through his head. Then, still frowning, he turned to look out the window again.

Amber was still bent over the file on the table in front of her, one arm propped on the tabletop, her hand supporting her head, her cloud of blonde hair spilling down around her shoulders. And it was perfectly obvious that she was so absorbed in her reading that she was totally unaware that anyone was watching her.

Zoltan's eyes drank her in, savouring every detail. The graceful curve of her neck, the soft sweep of her shoulders, the tantalising swell of her full, high breasts beneath the soft, flowing lines of the lilac-blue kaftan. He felt a tug of desire and found himself reflecting that she might look like an angel but she was definitely all woman. And a woman who, every time he looked at her, he simply desired more.

Fate was strange. He had brought her here because of the child. Because the child's need was great and because there was nothing he would not do for her. No other motive had been involved. He knew that to be true. And now, for the child's sake, she must be made to stay.

But whoever would have guessed that, while trying to save the child he loved, he would stumble upon so rare and wonderful a treasure? For though he had desired and won plenty of women over the years none had ever affected him, even remotely, as this one did. In her outspoken, spirited, independent way, she was by far the most exciting woman he had ever encountered in his entire life.

As she turned a page of the file, she shook her hair back from her shoulders, causing Zoltan to feel that thrust of desire again. And suddenly he remembered last night's dream.

He smiled. It had not surprised him that she had visited him in his dreams, for he was aware that she was fast turning into an obsession. But he had been surprised by the erotic intensity of his dream and by the crushing sense of loss and disappointment that had filled him when he had awakened with a start, his body burning like a torch, to discover that, after all, she was not lying there beside him, warm and naked, her sweet-scented flesh opening at his touch like a flower to receive him.

As he looked at her now, he felt again the agony of that moment and reflected that a man could only endure such dreams for so long. After a while, they started to make him crazy.

In the past, he had always prided himself on his powers of self-control, which were only equalled, it was often said, by his power to have what he desired, but he was growing more and more aware of a battle waging within him. With a fiercely growing urgency he longed to make love to her. And he had waited long enough. Now it was time to act.

As she leaned back in her chair and stretched for a moment, her breasts thrusting proudly against the thin fabric of her kaftan, he watched and quietly anticipated the not too far distant moment when the erotic pleasures of last night's dream would finally become reality.

And he was already planning when that might come about.

Tomorrow. At the Bedouin camp. Out in the desert, beneath the stars.

'Tape recorder, notepads, pencils and camera. Sun hat, sun cream, mosquito spray and moisturiser. Two pairs of trousers, three long-sleeved blouses, half a dozen changes of underwear and a pair of pyjamas.'

It was ten o'clock at night and, dressed in her cotton robe, Amber was ticking off her list before starting to pack for tomorrow's trip. But as she cast a critical eye over the neat piles of items spread out over the white silk coverlet of her bed she kept feeling that something essential was missing, though, according to her list, she had everything she was going to need.

'Make sure you're covered up as much as possible on trips to the desert,' she'd been advised by one of her female journalist friends whose regular patch was the Middle East. 'Wear trousers rather than shorts, in spite of the heat, loose, long-sleeved tops, shoes rather than sandals. And slap on the highest-factor sun screen you can find. At night, wear pyjamas, for it can suddenly get cold.

'And remember that, though the desert may be one of the most alluring places on earth, it also happens to be one of the most dangerous.'

Alluring and dangerous. Amber smiled wryly to herself. These adjectives were also a pretty good description of Sheikh Zoltan, which was probably why she kept having the feeling that something essential was missing from her list. What was missing was something to protect her from the wretched man!

Like a roll of barbed wire. That might prove rather more reliable than her own decidedly shaky powers of resistance. For she really hadn't been greatly impressed by these lately.

In the last couple of days since he'd told her about the trip, their paths, thank heavens, had crossed only a couple of times. But on both of those occasions the sad truth was that she'd behaved with about as much resolution as a blancmange.

Their first unfortunate encounter had been the other morning as Rashid was escorting her out to the car to take her to the first of her interviews in town. Quite suddenly, Sheikh Zoltan had appeared at the end of the corridor, sweeping along, robes billowing out behind him, clearly on his way to some appointment himself. And at the sight of him Amber had felt a quick, hot flare in her stomach.

Angry at herself, she'd shaken the feeling from her, but then it had happened again as he'd stopped to greet her and she'd found herself looking into those sensuous dark eyes.

'Good morning,' he said. 'I see you're on your way. I hope you have a fruitful day.'

'Thank you,' she answered, looking at him and not looking at him, desperately struggling to get herself back in control.

'I'm going to be busy for most of the day, but I'll try to see you some time this evening. I'll be extremely interested to know how you've got on.'

And then, before she could answer, he was sweeping off down the corridor again.

Amber cursed herself all morning for this pitiful showing on her part. What was happening to her brain? Not since she was about thirteen had she acted all tongue-tied and pathetic like this and it was starting to happen far too often with Sheikh Zoltan. But at least by the time she saw him again in the evening she was feeling rather more in charge of herself again.

The reason for that was mostly anger.

He walked into the dining room as she was finishing dinner on her own, enjoying a cup of the local coffee and a couple of delicious *halwa*, the sweets—similar to Turkish delight—which were always served with it. She glanced up at him and felt a quick, sharp dart of hostility mingled with a sense of perverse satisfaction. She'd been hoping he might appear, for she had a bone to pick with him.

'So, there you are,' he said, coming to stand before her. 'I'm sorry I was unable to join you for dinner, but I've only just managed to escape from a meeting. Still, I hope you enjoyed your meal and that everyone's been looking after you?'

'Yes, they have, thanks. And dinner was excellent,' she assured him.

There was a clipped edge to her tone; though, as she looked into his face, just for a moment she almost forgot her anger. His eyes held a troubled look, strangely naked, almost vulnerable. There was no sign at all of the usual indomitable self-assurance. And it caught her by surprise. He has something on his mind, she thought. Some intuition also told her that whatever it was was intensely personal.

How strange. She'd imagined that a man in his position, so rich, so privileged, so totally powerful, wouldn't have a single personal care in the world. But of course that was ridiculous, she realised as she thought about it. Being privileged didn't stop you being human.

As she looked at him, to her surprise she felt a tiny twinge of sympathy.

'Good. I'm glad my orders have been adhered to. Since I knew I wouldn't manage to join you this evening, I left instructions that you were to be given the very best treatment.'

As he spoke, he bent to pick up one of the silk cushions from the pile that lay on the near side of the table and tossed it onto the floor just a couple of feet away from her. Then, reaching out quickly to snatch a couple of fresh dates from the huge silver bowl of fruit on the table, he seated himself on the cushion and popped one of the dates into his mouth.

Amber watched him, privately observing two things. One, that he'd seated himself just a little too close for comfort. Two, that his troubled look had rather abruptly vanished. Back in place was the old familiar self-assurance. She felt a flicker of annoyance at herself for ever having felt sorry for him and a nice warm bubbling-up inside her of renewed anger.

And then, right on cue, he asked her, 'So, how did your interviews go?'

This was precisely the subject Amber had been planning to get round to. She told him,

'The interviews went extremely well. I got lots of information. Everyone was very helpful. However,' she continued, eyes narrowing as she looked at him, 'I'm afraid there was one rather unfortunate problem. . .'

'Really?' He popped the other date into his mouth. 'Tell me about it,' he invited.

'I intend to.'

Amber peered irritably across at him. There was something about the way he was sitting there looking at her that warned her he was not about to take her complaint terribly seriously. Letting him know that she did, she informed him in a clipped tone, 'The problem, I'm afraid, was Rashid.'

He stopped chewing. 'Rashid? I've never known Rashid to be a problem.' The black eyes looked at her with bemused curiosity. 'I think you'd better tell me what Rashid's been up to.'

'Oh, I'm not blaming Rashid.' Amber threw him a level look She had a great deal of time for his dignified, bearded servant and had no desire to get him into trouble. 'I've got no personal beef with Rashid. That's not what I was meaning. I'm quite sure he was only following orders.'

She paused, fixing him with a look that was sharp with accusation. The kind of look that would make most people shift in their seat. Sheikh Zoltan's response was to help himself to another couple of dates.

He put one in his mouth. 'You've got me curious now,' he said.

Amber took a deep breath. Boy, was he infuriating. It would serve him right if he choked on his damned date.

She continued, keeping her tone calm, 'I knew he was to accompany me to the interviews. I was aware that he was to sit in and act as interpreter. And he performed these two functions absolutely perfectly. . .'

She paused and snatched an exasperated breath. 'But what I didn't know was that he was going to be my shadow, refusing, even for a second, to let me out of his sight. At one point, while we were down town with about fifteen minutes to kill between appointments, I told him I felt like taking a short walk, just to have a look at some of the shops, and he refused point-blank to let me go off on my own, even though I made it perfectly clear that was what I wanted.'

She was aware that her voice had risen angrily as she demanded, 'Perhaps you can offer an explanation? If you can, I'd be really interested to hear it.' Her eyes crackled at him with annoyance. 'Quite frankly, I found it insufferable!'

Sheikh Zoltan watched her for a moment as though considering his answer.

'Didn't it occur to you,' he said at last, 'that he was simply looking after you? You're a young woman on your own in a country where you don't speak the language and where you are relatively unfamiliar with the customs. I would say you ought to be grateful to him, not angry at what he did.'

This was more or less the response that Amber had expected. She took a deep breath. 'Let's get one thing quite clear. I'm a grown woman, not a child, and I don't need a nanny. This isn't the first time I've been on my own in a foreign country and, believe it or not, I've always managed perfectly.

'So, if concern for my welfare is really what was behind all this. . .' she paused, making it plain that she didn't believe that for a moment '. . .then I'd like to assure you that it really isn't necessary. And I'd be grateful if, next time Rashid accompanies me some-where, you'd instruct him to give me a little more space.'

'More space?'

'Yes, more space. Is that too much to ask?' His unshakeable calmness was making her seethe. She fixed him with a flinty look. 'As I've already told you, I don't like being treated like a prisoner!'

As she'd half expected he would, he smiled at that. 'Ah,' he said, 'so we're back to that again. Why is it that every little thing that happens makes you feel you're being treated like a prisoner?'

'It's not *every* little thing. Don't try to accuse me of being neurotic. It's just things like suddenly finding my bedroom door locked and having somebody follow me about like a jailer, refusing to let me out of his sight for a second. Anyone having to put up with that would feel they were being treated like a prisoner!

'And another thing,' she added as he continued to

smile. 'That woman I told you about... I'm sure she's still spying on me.'

His smile instantly vanished. 'You saw her again? Where?' he demanded. 'When did this happen?'

'I didn't actually see her. It was this morning, when I was going to meet Rashid. I'm sure she was hiding in one of the doorways along the corridor. I could feel her eyes on me. I just knew she was there.'

Sheikh Zoltan cursed beneath his breath. 'This should not have happened,' he said. 'I apologise. It will not happen again.'

An apology from the great Sheikh? Unbelievable! Surely this must be as rare as a rainstorm in the desert?

'But don't let it worry you,' he continued. 'This person means you no harm. She is only being over-curious. You can take my word for it that there is no cause for concern.'

But who was she? Amber had a feeling it was important for her to know. But, just as she was about to ask, a different concern occurred to her.

She frowned into his face. 'Don't be hard on her, will you? I mean, you won't punish her? There's no need for that. As you just said yourself, she hasn't done me any harm.

'Just ask her to stop. That's all,' she added reasonably, for the woman's attentions definitely made her feel uncomfortable.

'Of course.' Sheikh Zoltan smiled. 'I shall restrict myself to having a quiet word with her.'

He watched her for a moment and then, as though on a sudden impulse, he reached out to smooth her brow with his fingers. Amber very nearly gasped. The touch of him was like fire.

'I shall also have a word with Rashid,' he continued. 'I shall tell him that, from now on, he must give you more space.'

He let his fingers slide down to caress her cheek softly, shooting flames across her skin and igniting deep inside her a helpless, hungry flare of desire. Then he smiled.

'But try to understand that he was only looking after you. All he was really guilty of was an excess of zeal.'

'I suppose so.'

It was the best that Amber could manage. She felt paralysed, scarcely able to breathe for the sudden wild excitement that roared in her veins.

'Happy now?'

As he spoke, he let his fingertips brush her mouth, pausing there for a moment, his eyes drifting down to them as, in response, her lips parted, hot needles rushing through her.

She nodded. She knew it would be pointless to try to speak.

'Good. But you must be sure to tell me at once if the woman bothers you again or if Rashid fails to give you space.' He smiled and held her eyes, the black gaze pouring over her. 'I want you to promise me that you will do that.'

He paused, waiting for her promise.

'I will.' A hoarse croak.

Amber's head was spinning. She could hardly even see straight. The only thing she could think about was whether or not he was going to kiss her.

Less than a millisecond later, she knew that he was.

His fingers slid from her mouth and, tangling softly with her hair, moved unhurriedly round to the back of her head. Then he was leaning towards her, drawing her closer, and it seemed to Amber that her heart was about to burst in the agonising second before his lips finally met hers.

When they did, the effect was like an explosion within her. A tumbling, unstoppable avalanche of sensation. With a sigh, she closed her eyes and let the avalanche pour over her. Her heart was clamouring inside her.

It was the softest, most sensuous, most unhurried kiss ever. But it crackled with fire. There was passion at its centre. It was a kiss that simmered softly with unspoken promises.

There was never any hope that Amber might fight it. At the touch of his lips, a stab of desire—fierce and unstoppable—had gone piercing right through her. She'd felt her whole body slacken. There'd been no choice but to receive him. To happily surrender and kiss him back.

Every inch of her was trembling as he drew away to look at her, and at the ferocity in the black eyes she felt herself shiver. It was a look that consumed her, that ate up her soul.

He said, smiling darkly, 'I think we understand each other now.' His fingers caressed her face, then trailed gently through her hair. 'Yes,' he said again. 'I think that we do.'

He kissed her once more, then, his eyes still holding hers, slowly he began to rise to his feet. 'I'm afraid I must leave you now. I still have things to do.'

Then, with a burning glance, he turned to leave the room.

Amber watched him go in a turmoil of confused emotion. She felt elated yet appalled at herself, her body weak with wanting him. Never before had she experienced anything like this.

At the doorway, he paused to cast her one last glance. And though she wasn't really sure what it was in his expression that triggered it—maybe just a hint of that troubled look of before—suddenly, in that instant, she understood something. She felt a quick, sharp, painful tug at her heart. Now she knew who the mystery woman was.

All of these things had happened last night and Amber had thought of little else since. Whether she'd been reading in the courtyard or doing interviews down town—fortunately, she hadn't set eyes on Sheikh Zoltan all day—they'd stayed with her like a tune she just couldn't shake out of her head. They were what she was thinking of now as she cast a last appraising glance over the items laid out over the bed, all ready for packing for the desert trip tomorrow.

That kiss, of course, had been a serious mistake—as well as pretty damning proof of her inability to resist him. She hadn't even tried. Quite the opposite. She'd kissed him back. Heaven only knew what he must be thinking now.

And that was what really worried her. The impression she'd given. No doubt he was imagining that that kiss was just the start, a sign that she was weakening and there was a great deal more to come.

Well, he couldn't be more wrong. She wasn't under his spell to that extent. There was no way she'd be tempted into a cheap, sordid affair.

Snatching up her flight bag, she began to dump her things inside. So, he was in for a disappointment if that was what he had in mind.

She pulled the zipper of the bag shut. Besides, it would be easy to resist him now. Now that she knew the truth there was no danger at all. What she knew was the perfect antidote to temptation.

For she was certain now that he'd lied. He'd told her he wasn't married and at the time she'd been unsure whether to believe him or not. But now, after last night, she was no longer unsure. Now she was convinced that he was married, after all.

That was the revelation that had suddenly come to her when he'd turned to look at her on his way out the door.

He was married, and the mystery woman who was spying on her was his wife.

CHAPTER NINE

'How about stopping to have some breakfast? We're making good time and I'm sure you could do with something to eat.'

Amber was torn. He was right. She was hungry. But a cosy little breakfast with him definitely didn't appeal. It would be wiser to encourage him to press ahead to the camp, where at least they'd be surrounded by other people.

'I'm not hungry,' she lied. 'Don't bother to stop on my account.'

Her lie was a waste of time. Sheikh Zoltan was stopping anyway.

'Well, your driver's a bit less stoical than you are,' he was saying. 'I'm afraid I've got to have something to eat.'

They'd been on the road for over an hour, since just after six-thirty when they'd met outside the palace. 'Better to travel early, before it gets too hot,' he'd told her, for the temperature rose much higher out in the desert, and the Bedouin camp was a couple of hours' drive away.

Once out of the palace gates, they'd headed straight for the new highway that cut like a wide asphalt gash through the desert, as though from out of the sky some huge sword had descended and in one mighty stroke had divided the land in two.

This was nothing like her first foray into the desert,

Amber had realised as they'd quickly left the city behind them. This was definitely no tourist desert. This was the real thing. A vast, seemingly endless, uninterrupted stretch of sand, like something out of *Lawrence of Arabia*. In the course of the last hour, they'd seen only one other car, travelling in the opposite direction, and the only road signs were warnings to beware of straying camels. This place was as deserted as the far side of the moon.

It was also every bit as intriguing, as her journalist friend had told her. Or it would have been if she'd been able to keep her mind on the landscape, for in spite of all her efforts to control them her thoughts kept straying to the dangerous, dark presence at her side.

In this huge, empty landscape she was entirely alone with him. Panic and excitement kept colliding inside her.

These feelings were pretty much entirely of her own making, for Sheikh Zoltan had done nothing in particular to stir them up. When they'd met at the appointed hour, he'd merely greeted her with a curt nod, making no attempt to kiss her as she'd been dreading he might. And so far throughout the journey he'd restricted his conversation to impersonal little nuggets of local information, explaining, for example, about the different desert seasons or how some particular sand-dune came to have a particular shape.

It was almost as though that kiss had never happened.

But it had happened and Amber knew he was as aware of it as she was. This show of detachment was nothing but a camouflage. She could feel, more strongly than ever, that electric tension between them, that sensation that something was sizzling just below the surface. But at least as long as they were speeding along the highway, he with his hands safely occupied by the steering wheel, she keeping her eyes steadfastly fixed out the window, it was just about possible to endure being cooped up with him like this. We'll be there soon, she kept telling herself. Safe and surrounded by other people.

But now he was drawing the big blue Range Rover to a halt out here in the middle of nowhere, pulling on the handbrake and removing his hands from the steering wheel, then turning to say something so she was obliged to swivel round and face him.

'I brought along a few things. Some coffee and fresh dates, as well as some bread and a couple of pastries.' He held her eyes for a moment. 'I really think you ought to eat something. It isn't very wise, you know, to travel on an empty stomach.'

'OK, I'll have something.'

She knew he was right and there wasn't much point in continuing to pretend she wasn't hungry. But, as he reached into the back seat for the picnic box, she quickly added, 'I think I'll get out. I'd like to stretch my legs for a couple of minutes.'

What she really wanted to do was put some distance between them. As she'd looked into his eyes, she'd felt the electricity between them surge. And she definitely didn't trust him, any more than she trusted herself. One kiss could lead to another. Then another. And then what? No, the only safe place was as far away from him as she could get.

As she pushed the car door open, she heard him warn her, 'I think you may find it a bit hot out there. You'd be better to eat in the car, or at least to put on a hat.'

Amber paid him no heed, though it was definitely

hotter than she'd expected—far hotter than it had ever
been in her shady courtyard at the palace. So it was true
what he'd told her about the heat of the desert.

Still, it was a great deal more comfortable than
staying in the car with him. 'Don't worry,' she told him,
a little annoyed at his interference. 'A few minutes in
the sun won't do me any harm.' And, climbing down
from the car, she stepped to the edge of the road and
gazed out over the seemingly endless desert that surrounded them.

There really was something quite spectacular about
this place. The vast, shimmering silence, the light as
bright as crystal, the soft, earthy colours of the gently
rippling sand-dunes against the stark, almost violent
blue of the sky. She breathed in and let the strange,
harsh magic of it embrace her. This place was as old and
unchanging as time.

'Coffee.'

She turned to see that he'd moved over into the
passenger seat and was holding out a steaming plastic
cup.

'Thanks.'

Amber accepted it without looking directly at him,
and took a quick, grateful sip of the strong, sweet brew.
It was the special Arab coffee, scented with cardamom,
that she was very rapidly acquiring a taste for. And it
struck her, as he proceeded now to offer her the plastic
picnic box with its containers of fresh dates and bread
rolls and pastries, that it ought to feel strange to have
him looking after her like this. Pouring her coffee.
Handing her her breakfast. It ought to feel strange, but
inexplicably it didn't.

The quince.

As she chose a pastry and handed the box back to him, suddenly she remembered the business with the quince and instantly understood why none of this felt strange. But it had done her no good to recall that erotic episode. A quick, fierce jolt of excitement went rushing through her and that, in turn, reminded her of that kiss the other night. The most staggeringly mind-blowing kiss of her entire life.

Abruptly, she switched her gaze back to the desert and, taking a quick bite of her pastry, fished in her mind for something safe to say. Something to cancel out all those disturbing, unwanted thoughts.

A question occurred to her.

'Why did you insist on leaving so early, before it got too hot? I mean, what does the heat matter when you're travelling in an air-conditioned car?'

What had triggered that demand was undoubtedly the fact that he'd left the air-conditioning running and she could feel the draught from the car deliciously cool against her back.

'Surely,' she insisted, 'it makes no difference? Surely you could travel at midday if you wanted?'

'Yes, I suppose you could. But only if you had total faith.'

Amber frowned and cast a curious glance at him. 'I don't understand. Total faith in what?'

'Total faith in the car. Total faith that nothing can go wrong.'

'Like what?'

'Like the air-conditioning failing, for a start. Or—the worst scenario—the car itself breaking down.' The dark eyes were serious. 'Have you any idea,' he asked her, 'how long you would survive if you were stranded out here in the midday sun?'

Amber hadn't thought of that. 'Not very long, I suppose. Unless you had plenty of water, you'd die of dehydration pretty fast.'

'In the summer, without water, you'd last less than a couple of days. Even at this time of the year, you wouldn't last a great deal longer.' As she frowned, he smiled. 'But don't worry,' he told her. 'I always carry plenty of water in the back of the car.'

It was a chastening thought. Amber swivelled her gaze round again to the empty, shimmering, endlessly stretching sand. 'And there was I just thinking how beautiful it all was,' she said.

'It is beautiful. But, like a beautiful woman, it is not to be trusted.'

As he paused, Amber sensed he was just waiting for her to turn and glare at him. She decided not to disappoint him.

He met her scowl with an unrepentant smile and continued, 'Like a beautiful woman, the desert is notoriously treacherous and fickle.'

'And what is that supposed to mean?' Something told her it had been personal.

She was right. It had been.

With a provocative glint in his eye, he put to her, 'Surely you of all people are bound to agree that beautiful women tend to be treacherous and fickle?'

He was referring, of course, to what she'd told him about her and Adrian. About how she'd broken off their engagement. But Amber had no desire to be pushed into having to defend herself, so she kept her answer strictly impersonal.

'I'm afraid I don't agree. Surely no one could believe that women have the monopoly on fickleness and treachery? I'd say that in those fields men hold most of the prizes.'

He neither agreed nor disagreed. He simply switched the conversation back to personal.

'So, this fiancé of yours betrayed you? Is that what you're telling me? That would explain why you suddenly changed your mind about marrying him.'

Amber knew when she was cornered. She tilted her head and faced him.

'My fiancé did not betray me.' Her voice was calm and unemotional. Then, just to stop him asking any more questions, she elaborated, 'I changed my mind because it would have been a mistake for us to marry. I came to realise that the two of us simply weren't suited.'

As she said it, she was aware of not feeling defensive at all, rather of being filled with a sense of total certainty. No more guilt. No more doubts. No more heart-searching. It really was that simple, after all. In spite of what all her friends had kept telling her, she'd been absolutely right to break off the engagement. It was the sanest, most sensible thing she'd ever done.

She'd always known it in her heart, but this was the first time she'd been able to say it and feel totally at peace with her decision. It was like a weight off her shoulders. She could breathe easy again. Though she wondered why this emotional breakthrough should suddenly have happened now.

But, all at once, something else was causing her rather more concern. Just a touch of light-headedness as she stood there in the sun. She stepped nearer to the open car door and leaned against it as she added, just to make sure he fully understood the point she'd been making. 'The way I acted was neither fickle nor treacherous. On the contrary, it was responsible. What I did was best for both of us.'

She finished off her pastry and washed it down with the rest of her coffee. Perhaps she'd feel better with a bit of sustenance inside her.

'Would your fiancé agree with that? It must have been rather hard on him.' He paused, letting his eyes trail unhurriedly over her. 'Losing a beautiful girl like you must have been a bit of a blow.'

Amber ignored that look and answered his question. 'Yes, as a matter of fact, I think he probably would agree. And, one day, he'll meet a girl who'll make him far happier than I could have done.'

'I see. You were simply being cruel to be kind?'

The mockery in his tone angered her. Talk about the pot calling the kettle black!

Amber fixed him with a look that made it plain what she was getting at. 'Whatever you may think, I never betrayed him. I never lied to him or was unfaithful. . . That, in my opinion, would have been treachery.'

She was about to stop there, but couldn't resist adding, 'But no doubt you have rather different standards on such matters?'

As she spoke, she leaned a little more heavily against the car door and was aware that she was having to concentrate rather hard on holding onto her empty coffee cup. Suddenly, she was feeling distinctly odd.

Sheikh Zoltan had clearly picked up her discomfort. He frowned into her flushed face. 'Why don't you come and sit in the shade?' With a flick of his hand he indicated the sill of the car. 'You really shouldn't stand out in the sun like that.'

'Don't worry. I'm fine.' Amber dismissed the invitation. The sill was far too unappealingly close to him. She'd far sooner fry than go and sit there. Besides, she was irritated at the way he'd avoided her question.

She put it a different way. 'You don't believe in honesty and fidelity, do you?'

'Don't I? And what makes you say that?' he countered.

Amber noted that he sounded amused—not guilty, as he ought to have done. But that shouldn't surprise her. Guilt probably wasn't in his repertoire.

She fixed him with a sabre-sharp look. 'Your behaviour makes me say it. Let me put it frankly. . . You told me you weren't married. But now I happen to know that you are.'

'Do you, indeed? And to whom am I married?' He still sounded amused, but at least he hadn't denied it.

'I don't know who all your wives are, but I suspect that one of them is that woman. That woman who's been spying on me. The one I told you about. My guess is that she's wondering what the devil I'm doing here. Maybe she's jealous or something. And I imagine she probably has good cause to be. Though, naturally, not of me,' she amended quickly. 'She'll never have any cause to be jealous of me.'

'You think not?'

'I'm very sure of it.'

'Personally, I suspect you may be mistaken.'

'I can assure you I'm not. You're the one who's mistaken.'

As she spoke, she had to close her eyes and breathe slowly. All at once, her head was swimming.

Fighting the sensation, she threw him a warning look, for there was an intense look on his face that was making her nervous.

'I think it's important that you understand what I'm saying and don't get the wrong idea about the other night—'

Amber stopped as he began to climb down from the car. His face was going in and out of focus and she couldn't make out a word he was saying. As she continued to fight for breath, he was coming towards her.

She pressed back against the car door as sudden panic rose inside her. Everything seemed to be slipping out of control.

'I mean it,' she warned him. 'You'd better believe me. As long as I have the strength to fight you off, there'll never be a repetition of what happened the other night.'

Then her legs turned to powder and she slumped helplessly to the ground.

Amber was aware of being gathered up into a pair of strong arms. She felt weightless. Suspended. As though she was floating. Unresisting, she sank against him. It was the most beautiful sensation.

He was carrying her to the car. Her head was resting on his shoulder, and the virile, hard strength of him felt comforting and secure. Never in her life had she felt so protected. And it was strange, the total sense of belonging that she felt.

He was reclining the car seat and laying her down. The soft leather felt cool and welcoming against her back. And he was saying something as he bent over her, his tone gentle and reassuring.

'Don't worry, *habibiti*. I'll look after you.'

With light, delicate fingers, he brushed back her hair. 'How beautiful you are,' Amber thought she heard him say. As she looked up at him, she was tempted to answer, So are you.

He had pushed the white *kaffiyeh* back from his face, so that it formed a frame for his strong, masculine features. Those black eyes like whirlpools, with their amazingly long, thick lashes, the strong nose that lent his face its proud, noble character, and that mouth that was capable of inflicting such intense pleasure. Amber looked at that mouth and longed to feel its magic again.

'Here. Drink some of this.'

He was holding a cup to her lips, his other hand gently supporting her shoulders. Amber drank, though all she was aware of was his scent in her nostrils. Delicious. Intoxicating. Making her heart race.

She was half-aware of his hand on the top button of her high-necked blouse. She half heard him say, 'I think we ought to loosen this.' Then it seemed to her that she sighed and tried to reach out to touch his hair, though she wasn't at all sure whether she actually did so or not.

Reality was slipping away. She was falling into a dream.

In the dream, she could feel the brush of his hair against her fingers and it was every bit as soft and silky as she'd imagined. With a smile, holding her breath, she ran her fingers through it, while with her other hand she reached up and softly caressed his face.

It was at that point in her dream that he bent to kiss her, lips burning like fire, making her gasp and press against him. And as his mouth moved over hers she could feel his hand on her breast as he began to undo the remaining buttons of her blouse. She shivered and held her breath till the final button was undone and, at last, the front of her blouse fell open.

'*Habibiti! Habibiti!*'

She could hear the words, like music, as he pushed aside her bra and took hold of her breasts, hands moulding the firm flesh, fingers brushing the thrusting nipples, sending shockwaves of sensation, like electric pulses, tearing through her. Her desire felt as tight as a clenched fist inside her. Never in all her life had she wanted a man like this.

As she lay there, throbbing, he was undoing the belt at her waist. She closed her eyes, arms embracing him, as he stripped her trousers away.

Then, at last, she was naked, and he was throwing off his own clothes. Amber watched in breathless wonder as he slowly revealed himself. Every smooth, virile line of his hard-muscled body—the broad athlete's chest with its sprinkling of fine black hairs, the flat, hard-as-iron plane of his stomach, the wide, muscular shoulders, the powerful thighs—was a brazen invitation to sensory pleasure. And one that Amber had no desire to resist.

As he kissed her and caressed her, hands touching and exploring, whipping the excitement inside her to a storm, she in turn let her hands enjoy every inch of him, giving pleasure for pleasure and taking pleasure in the giving. And it felt as though this new intimacy between them had always been.

Their bodies were still two, but already they felt as one, fused by the age-old, universal rhythms of their desire. For what was happening between them was greater than the two of them. As ancient and as timeless as the desert that surrounded them.

That was Amber's last thought as her dream began to evaporate at precisely the moment when their two bodies became one.

CHAPTER TEN

'WELCOME back to the land of the living. So, how are you feeling now?'

Amber opened her eyes and blinked, wondering for a moment where she was. She was lying flat on her back on the passenger seat of the Range Rover, which had been adjusted to provide a remarkably comfortable bed, and sitting right next to her at the wheel was Sheikh Zoltan.

He smiled down at her, shifting his eyes for a moment from the road. 'You've been sleeping,' he told her. 'Probably the best thing you could have done. And now, you'll be pleased to hear, we're nearly at the camp.'

'I've been sleeping?'

'Don't you remember? You suffered a bit of sunstroke. We were right in the middle of the most fascinating conversation when suddenly you turned as white as a sheet and keeled over.'

It was all coming back to her as Amber started to sit up, snapping up the back of her seat behind her. She'd been accusing him of lying about not being married, telling him she knew that the mystery woman was his wife and warning him that as long as she had the strength to fight him there'd never be a repetition of that kiss the other night.

But what had happened next? She felt a rush of alarm as her hand flew to her neck and found the top button of her blouse undone.

'I'm afraid I did that.' Sheikh Zoltan threw her an amused look. 'Loosening the patient's clothing is standard procedure when someone passes out the way you did. I'm afraid I also loosened your belt and the waistband of your trousers and helped you take a drink of water. Fortunately, no more drastic measures were called for.'

Long before he'd come to the end of this explanation, Amber had turned away to stare fixedly out the window, though of the speeding desert landscape she made out not a thing.

'That was good of you,' she acknowledged, still without a glance at him. For a blush as fiery red as the desert sun at sunset was creeping up her face from her neck to her hairline.

Suddenly, to her horror, she was remembering in vivid detail that erotic dream she'd had while she'd been sleeping. Sheikh Zoltan making love to her. Her making love to him. At the memory she felt her whole body burn.

She must have been delirious, she told herself defensively. How else could she have dreamt such an utterly outrageous thing?

'You were asleep for quite a while and, like I said, we're almost there now.' He glanced at his watch. 'Another fifteen minutes or so.'

'Good.'

Amber still couldn't bring herself to look at him. How would she ever be able to look him in the face again? She kept thinking of how he'd looked in his virile nakedness in her dream. The thrill of him touching her. The excitement of touching him. And it must show in her eyes. He'd guess at her lewd thoughts.

She stared hard at the fleeing landscape. Thank

heavens we're almost there, she thought. The sooner we arrive and I can get out of the car, the sooner I'll be able to control this wretched madness and the sooner this whole miserable ordeal will be over.

Let's just hope I survive it, she silently prayed, with my sanity—and everything else—intact.

The Bedouin encampment appeared quite suddenly, nestling in the midst of a scatter of palm trees.

'We're here,' Sheikh Zoltan announced as they headed towards it. And Amber felt a plummet of relief in her heart.

They'd turned off the main road five or six miles back and then had driven across the sand, apparently at random, for there were neither road nor road signs, nor any sign of life. Not that Amber had felt concerned. She trusted him totally—at least she did when it came to navigating the desert, for she sensed he knew it like the back of his hand. She was relieved, quite simply, because now they'd no longer be alone.

Far from it, by the looks of things! As the Range Rover drew to a halt, from out of every corner, from the mouths of tents and from under palm trees, a positive throng of people descended on them. Old men, young men, women and children, all hurrying towards them and calling out in welcome.

'That's quite a reception committee,' Amber commented, impressed.

'For you.' He smiled back at her. 'You're a very special guest.'

Quite possibly that was part of it, Amber decided as they climbed down from the car and introductions were made. Their hosts certainly couldn't have made her feel more welcome. But, all the same, she wasn't fooled. It

was perfectly obvious that the one they were really
delighted to see was Sheikh Zoltan.

And he was being greeted like a good friend rather
than a ruler. Amber hadn't expected that and she felt
just a little thrown.

She was introduced first of all to the head of the tribe,
a striking looking man by the name of Abu Bakar, and
then, one by one, to the senior members of his family.
None of them spoke any English, but no translation was
really necessary for her to appreciate how warmly she
was being gathered into their midst.

'*Shokrun. Shokrun,*' she told them, feeling rather glad
that at least she'd learned the Arabic for thank you!

It was as she was being ushered into the chief's tent
once the introductions were over that Amber suddenly
noticed, standing near the back of the crowd, the old
man she'd seen that day in the library. So, she'd been
wrong when she'd wondered if, in spite of his shabby
clothes, he might, after all, be someone important and
that was why Sheikh Zoltan had been so polite to him.
That clearly wasn't the case, for she'd already been
introduced to all the senior members of the tribe.

She was just thinking this when Sheikh Zoltan suddenly detached himself from the group and went hurrying over to greet the old man.

Amber watched as, just like that other time, he laid a
hand on his arm and bent to exchange a couple of words
with him. How strange. What was he saying to him and
who could the old man be?

Inside the tent, where Sheikh Zoltan came to join her
a minute or two later, the floor was strewn with
colourful tribal rugs on which everyone proceeded to
seat themselves, cross-legged. Amber and Sheikh

Zoltan, as guests of honour, sat down in the centre of the group, next to the chief and the other elders, as some women appeared bearing glasses of sweet tea and trays piled high with freshly picked dates and, smiling broadly, proceeded to offer them round.

'As you know,' Sheikh Zoltan told her, 'it is an old Arab custom to welcome guests with food and drink. It is a tradition that, like most traditions, has practical roots. A traveller in the desert is sure to be hungry and thirsty. By offering hospitality to those who happen our way, we ensure that we, in turn, will receive the same good treatment.'

Amber listened, remembering how, when she'd first arrived at the palace, he'd insisted on offering her that amazing mini-banquet. When she'd tried to decline his hospitality, pretending to be concerned that for him it was a waste of time, he'd said that time taken to observe his country's customs was never wasted, though she hadn't really realised the significance of that claim then. She'd been too busy worrying what evil he might be plotting!

It felt as if a lifetime had passed since then. As she looked at him now, it was hard to believe that it had only been a few days ago. Sometimes he still scared her and he constantly surprised her, but he no longer felt like the threatening stranger he'd been then. At times, like now, she even felt a fragile bond with him.

'They have a similar code in the Highlands,' she told him. 'That's the northern part of Scotland where my father's ancestors come from. It's such a deeply ingrained custom that in times gone by a man would even offer hospitality to a traveller he suspected of being an enemy.'

Sheikh Zoltan watched her with interest. 'These Highlanders of yours are clearly Arab Bedouin at heart.'

'Or vice versa,' Amber countered, smiling back at him. 'Perhaps your Arab Bedouin are Highlanders at heart.' Foolishly, she found the notion rather pleasing.

Several cups of tea and handfuls of fresh dates later, the official welcoming ceremony was over.

'Nabila will show you to your tent now,' Sheikh Zoltan told Amber as a pretty young woman suddenly appeared beside them. 'She will also show you where you can have a shower if you feel like freshening up before getting down to some interviews or whatever you want to do first.'

'That sounds perfect.' She felt sticky from the heat and rather urgently in need of a shower and a change of clothes. 'I'll be as quick as I can and then, if it's OK, I'd like to speak to some of the women.'

'Whatever you want. Naturally, I shall be at your disposal—as interpreter or if you just need someone to explain things. Though I shall endeavour, of course,' he added with an amused look, 'since I know how important it is to you, to give you plenty of space.'

Amber smiled to herself over this remark later in the shower—not really a shower at all, of course, just a basic arrangement with a large bucket of water and a hand-carved wooden scoop, though it did the job perfectly adequately. It was quite a step forward for him to be making jokes like that! And, fortunately, she appeared to have recovered from her shameful dream and felt able to look him in the face again without blushing. Perhaps this trip was going to be quite civilised, after all.

It also looked as though it was going to be safe and seduction-free!

The sleeping arrangements had put her mind at rest. Her tent, which was sparsely but comfortably furnished with just a narrow tressle-bed and a wooden stool, was on the edge of a group where some of the women slept—mostly widowed grandmothers or young girls without husbands. Sheikh Zoltan's tent, if she'd understood correctly from Nabila, was on the other side of the encampment, with the men. It felt deeply reassuring to have this distance between them.

The day that followed was packed and utterly intriguing. First, Amber spent a couple of hours with some of the women, who told her through her efficient and remarkably unobtrusive interpreter the various day-to-day details of their lives—how they cooked, what they cooked, the way they raised their children, the crafts they excelled in that had been handed down through the generations—rug-making and weaving and the most exquisite embroidery.

They showed her, too, the ancient, traditional use of henna, employed mostly to paint intricate designs on their hands. Amber was enthralled and filled two whole tapes on her tape recorder.

They stopped for a quick lunch and a short siesta. Though Amber didn't sleep. She sat on her bed and scribbled notes. Then, although it was hot, she left her tent and wandered round the camp for a while, just looking at things and taking photographs. There was so much to see and learn in this place that she was loath to waste a single second.

She was standing at the edge of the encampment, looking out to the desert as she snapped a group of camels that had wandered off a little, when she suddenly became aware of a pair of eyes on her. She swung round, knowing instantly whom she would see.

Sheikh Zoltan smiled at her. 'I'm glad that at least you put on a hat.'

'Of course.' Amber smiled back at him and patted the sun hat on her head. 'I try not to make the same mistake twice.' To her surprise, she felt rather pleased to see him.

That probably had something to do with this morning, for the time they'd spent together had been totally harmonious. As well as being unobtrusive, he'd been helpful in the extreme, even offering suggestions as to whom she might be interested in speaking to and seeming to understand exactly what sort of information she was after. It seemed highly unlikely, but they'd made a good team.

Still, that reference to her sunstroke had instantly triggered other memories. The memory of his naked body pressed erotically against hers, his lips, his hands touching her as he'd made love to her in her dream.

Feeling a flush start to rise up, Amber quickly turned away again and pretended to be studying the group of camels she'd been snapping.

'I reckon camels must be the haughtiest looking animals in the world.'

She said it, really, just for something to say, to let him know she wasn't intending to be rude.

'They always have this air of looking down their noses at you,' she continued. 'And the haughty way they walk. . . That long-legged saunter. As though nothing in the world could induce them to hurry.'

'They can move if they have a mind to. They can run

almost as fast as a horse. While you're here in Ras al-Houht you ought to try and see a camel race. Then you'd see how fast they can go.'

Amber smiled. That idea rather appealed to her, though, of course, she probably wouldn't have time. What a pity, she thought fleetingly, that I'm not staying a little longer.

She glanced at the camels again. 'Why do they hobble them?' she asked. Their front legs were loosely tied together at the ankles.

'To stop them straying too far. And so that, if they do stray, they can be easily caught. It's a little hard to run with your front legs tied together.'

As she flicked a look at him again, he added with a smile, 'As you know, we're experts at stopping things from straying. You could say that hobbling is the camel equivalent of a locked door.'

Amber laughed. 'Well, I'm glad you didn't try to hobble me.' As she met his eyes, it crossed her mind how nice it was to be so relaxed with him. And how natural it felt. As though it had always been this way.

Maybe the aggro between them had just been due to a few crossed wires. Though maybe also to a bit of prejudice on her part, for at the beginning she'd been so ready to believe the worst of him all the time. Not once had she given him the benefit of the doubt. That suddenly made her think of the old man.

She cast him a curious look. 'Who is that old man? The one you spoke to when we first arrived here. The one we bumped into that day in the library.'

For a moment, he simply frowned at her, clearly surprised at the question. ' Just an old man,' he told her.

'His name is Saleh Ali.' The black eyes fixed on hers. 'Why did you want to know?'

'I just wondered. You seem to have a lot of time for him. And he's just an old man, isn't he? I mean, no one important?'

Sheikh Zoltan shrugged and shook his head. 'No, you're right, he's no one important. At least, not important in the way that you mean. Saleh Ali is just a poor old man with a problem. His grandson is seriously ill and the doctors here are unable to help him. The operation that can save his life can only be performed in London. He came to the palace to ask for my assistance.'

Amber was watching him carefully, reading between the lines. By 'assistance' he almost certainly meant financial help and probably also a hand in organising the whole thing.

'And were you able to help?' she asked.

Sheikh Zoltan nodded. 'The little boy has already been flown to London with his parents. He is due to be operated on tomorrow.'

He turned away, clearly wishing to change the subject. 'But I think it's time we got back to work now. You said you wanted to speak to some of the men this afternoon?'

Amber followed him as he led her back into the encampment, not sure if she was glad or sorry to know what she'd just learned. For some instinct was telling her he did this sort of thing a lot—doling out generous assistance to his subjects.

Where now was the uncaring tyrant she'd so despised?

* * *

'*Shokrun*, Nabila. I'll see you tomorrow. Goodnight.'

Amber kissed the girl's cheek and gave her a warm hug as they bade each other goodnight at the door of Amber's tent. Nabila had brought her a jug of drinking water as she'd been getting ready for bed and had been at pains to enquire if there was anything else she needed. It was amazing what you could communicate via sign language when you tried!

As Nabila disappeared out into the star-filled night, Amber stepped back inside and let the tent flap fall closed. It was only nine o'clock, but she was already dressed for bed, in her sensible pink and white striped pyjamas, for she was tired after a long, eventful day. Besides, tomorrow everyone would be up at the crack of dawn—people went to bed and got up with the sun in these parts—so it would be wise to get her head down straight away.

It was as she was kicking off her sandals that she suddenly noticed a square of bright blue cotton lying on the ground. It looked like a handkerchief. Amber bent to pick it up. Nabila must have dropped it. She'd give it to her in the morning.

But, at that moment, she heard a movement outside the tent flap.

Talk about coincidence! Amber turned round with a smile. 'Come in!' she called out, thinking it was Nabila come back for her hankie.

But it wasn't Nabila. Amber felt her smile falter as a tall dark figure dressed all in white, his black eyes like whirlpools, stepped into the tent.

'What are you doing here? What do you want?' She felt herself stiffen as the tent flap closed behind him. 'I thought you were Nabila. I didn't realise it was you.'

Alarm whipped through her, though it was tempered with quick excitement and with a perfectly inexcusable feeling of regret that she wasn't wearing something a little more glamorous than striped pyjamas!

Sheikh Zoltan paused for a moment with a look in his eyes that suggested he wasn't at all put off by her attire, causing Amber to change her mind hurriedly and decide it was just as well she was dressed the way she was. If he reacted like this to her frumpy cotton pyjamas, the effect of silk and lace just didn't bear thinking about!

He said with a small smile, 'I'm sorry I'm not Nabila. I came here, though it's late and I'm sure you want to get to sleep, because there's something I want to say and I think it's important.'

In the light from the gas lamp that stood on the floor by the bed throwing flat black shadows against the tent walls, he looked like some genie that had just sprung out of a bottle and was about to perform some mysterious magic.

But what kind of magic? Her stomach tightened at the thought.

'Oh, and what might that be?' Guilt made her tone sharp. She was totally mad to be thinking such thoughts. 'I can't imagine what could be so important that you have to come and tell me now.'

The black eyes looked down at her, flashing like diamonds in the lamplight. 'It concerns a conversation we had earlier,' he told her. 'When we stopped to have breakfast on our way here. Just before the heat finally got to you.'

Every allusion to that episode was guaranteed to unravel her. Amber scowled, fighting the blush she could feel rising to her cheeks. 'I'm sorry,' she told him, her tone positively clipped now, 'but I'm afraid I don't remember what we were talking about.'

It was the truth. All she could remember was the dream she'd had afterwards. And this definitely wasn't the moment to be remembering that. She was having trouble enough controlling her thoughts as it was.

'We were talking about that woman. The one you were upset about spying on you.' He paused and frowned into her face for a moment. 'You said you thought she was my wife. I want you to know that she is not.'

Amber blinked. This announcement was the last thing she'd been expecting.

'There's something else,' he went on. 'I told you I wasn't married. That happens to be the truth, though you may find it surprising. I don't even have one wife, let alone the harem you seem to think I have.'

His eyes flickered over her face. 'I think it's important that we get that straight.'

Amber didn't ask why he thought it was important. She suspected she already knew the answer to that. The question she didn't know the answer to was, did she believe him?

She made no effort to move away as he took a sudden step towards her. And she remained perfectly still as he reached out to touch her face. His fingers cupped her chin, sending a small shiver through her.

'I hope you believe me,' he said, his tone earnest.

Amber took a deep breath and met the dark gaze, feeling the touch of him turn her limbs to water. She nodded. The truth was that, at that precise moment, she'd have believed the earth was flat if he'd said so.

Besides, a voice was telling her, you've been wrong

about him so many times. Just for once, try trusting him. Give him the benefit of the doubt.

Sheikh Zoltan continued to look down at her, fingers clasped around her chin. 'Good,' he went on. 'I'm glad that's sorted out.'

As his eyes raked her face, Amber knew he was about to kiss her. But when he did it was the briefest, most fleeting of kisses. Over almost before it had begun.

She felt a hungry lurch inside her. Please don't stop, she wanted to say.

But he was stepping away. 'You're tired. I'll leave you now.'

Then he was crossing to the tent flap and snatching it up. But as he stepped outside he paused to glance up at the sky.

'So many stars,' he said. 'Did you ever see so many stars?' As she watched him, he turned to look at her again. 'Tomorrow night,' he told her, 'we will look at the stars together and I shall reveal to you all the secrets of an Arabian sky.'

Amber looked back at him, feeling a pulse start to beat in her throat.

'What if there are no stars tomorrow night?' she asked.

His eyes melted into hers. 'Oh, there will be,' he promised her. 'All the stars you could possibly need. I guarantee it.'

Then with a last dark flash of his eyes he was gone, leaving Amber standing staring at the tent flap through which he'd vanished, wondering, though in her heart she knew very well, exactly what that strange exchange had been about.

CHAPTER ELEVEN

AMBER spent much of the following day checking the sky for stars and trying to figure out whether or not she'd gone mad.

For one thing, even in Arabia the stars didn't come out in the daytime, and for another—and this was the real proof of her madness!—how could she even be contemplating falling into bed with Sheikh Zoltan?

For that was what they'd been talking about with all that subterfuge about stars. And she needn't try to kid herself that what they'd be doing was making love. Love didn't come into it. It would just be plain, lustful sex.

There'd be no emotion involved. No affection. No caring. Just the sating of hunger. The physical joining of two bodies. And, after a few short days, the whole thing would be over and she'd return to her life in London as though they'd never even met.

Was that what she wanted? A squalid little affair? Hadn't she always told herself she'd run a mile from something like that?

Yet the pull of him was so strong. As they spent another day together—as yesterday, working as two harmonious parts of a team—sometimes she would look at him and almost feel her heart fail. And it seemed to her that his effect on her was far more than just physical, as though there was some quality in him that reached right down into her soul.

140

Maybe that was why she'd always found him so unsettling.

Or was she just fooling herself, trying to justify her desires? That question, too, spun round endlessly in her brain. Perhaps she was talking herself into something that she'd only end up bitterly regretting?

Just stay calm, she told herself. You haven't committed yourself yet. Try to keep a clear head and wait and see what happens. When the moment finally comes and you have to make up your mind, you'll know in your heart the right thing to do.

The day passed more slowly than any Amber could remember, and yet, at the same time, it went by in a flash. Suddenly, the sun was going down in the sky, a ball of red fire melting the horizon, and in the encampment, where during the worst heat of the day life had virtually come to a stop, people were milling about, chatting and attending to their chores.

And, though there was still no sign of any stars, the moon hung like a pale, shadowy harbinger in the sky.

'I hope you're feeling up to a bit of a celebration tonight.'

As they finished the last interview and Amber switched off her tape recorder, Sheikh Zoltan glanced across at her with a smile.

Amber looked back at him, feeling a hungry clench inside her. It was hopeless. With every single second that passed, the thought of what lay ahead obsessed her more and more.

Though you haven't actually decided yet, she reminded herself.

'What kind of a celebration?' she asked him.

The dark eyes surveyed her. 'A very special celebration. You're to be the guest of honour at a grand
farewell dinner. An honour, I'd like to point out, that is
not bestowed on everyone.'

They were sitting in the rug-strewn tent of Abu
Bakar. Amber had decided to keep her interview with
him till last and it had turned out to be a worthy climax
to the last two days, for the chief of the tribe had
provided some perfect gems of information.

Amber glanced across at him now, as he sat between
her and Sheikh Zoltan. 'Please tell him I'm truly
honoured,' she replied. She felt deeply touched by this
unexpected gesture.

She was also glad to have something else other than
the stars for her mind to focus on! Inwardly, she sighed
with nervous relief. The dinner would give her a bit of
very welcome breathing-space.

There was only one small problem. Back in her tent,
as she started getting ready for the evening, it struck
Amber that she had nothing even remotely formal to
wear. All she'd brought with her were trousers and
cotton shirts. Next to the Bedouin women all decked
out in their finery—for she'd noticed that in private,
when they shed their black *chadors*, they had a taste for
striking, brightly coloured clothes—she was going to
look totally and utterly drab.

And then an inspired thought struck her: I'll speak to
Nabila!

Perhaps Nabila, having seen the modest contents of
Amber's travelling bag, had already been thinking the
same thing herself, for she understood instantly what
Amber was trying to tell her.

'Wait,' she told her, signalling her meaning. 'I'll bring something for you.'

Fifteen minutes later, Nabila reappeared through the tent flap, carrying over her arm a positive bonanza of dresses. They were all the sort of thing Amber wouldn't normally have dreamt of wearing—in bright, vivid colours, with elaborate embroidery—but she took one glance and knew they were exactly right for this evening.

She tried on half a dozen in different colours, but opted in the end for the first one that had caught her eye—a high-necked, long-sleeved semi-fitted kaftan in deep, bright turquoise with accents of pink and green. Examining herself in the small mirror that Nabila had brought with her, she laughed with delight and had to agree with her friend's verdict.

'*Jamila jiddan!*' Very beautiful!

It wasn't until she walked into Abu Bakar's tent and saw the flare in Sheikh Zoltan's eyes as he turned round to look at her that Amber realised she was wearing the dress partly for him. She felt a strange jolt inside her. Maybe she'd been unwise. Perhaps he would take this as a sign of capitulation. But though these thoughts went through her head it was only for a second. Not for anything would she have traded that look in his eyes.

He came and stood before her.

'I thought I must be dreaming.' He reached out one hand and touched her hair for a moment, sending a tingle of awareness from her scalp to her toes. 'Never in my life have I seen a woman half as beautiful.'

Amber blushed, feeling a little foolish. This is madness, she was thinking. What am I getting into? I must be out of my head.

For this was mere seduction. She was well aware of that. But as he took her by the hand and led her to the low brass table, where Abu Bakar and the principal guests would sit, she really didn't care if it was madness or not. If it was madness, then it was the most wonderful madness in the world. And she wasn't going to fight it any longer. Instead, she was simply going to relax and enjoy it!

The meal was a kaleidoscope of smells and tastes and colours. Dish after amazing dish was brought to the table. Mutton and rice and vegetables and salads. Dates and sweetmeats and figs stuffed with almonds. It was a farewell dinner she would never forget.

But the real cause of the excitement she could feel flushing her cheeks and filling her eyes with a magical sparkle was the man seated across from her at the other side of Abu Bakar, the man in the white robes, with the whirlpool-black gaze, who kept glancing across at her, making her heart race.

For there was no longer even a shred of doubt in her mind now. She'd never wanted anything more and nothing was going to stop her. There was a chance she'd regret it afterwards, of course, but she'd also regret it if she denied herself. And, anyway, it would take more strength than she possessed to say no.

At long last, the meal was drawing to a close. Coffee had been served, along with the traditional *halwa*, and Amber could feel the tension in her twist like a knife. Though it was the most exquisite kind of tension. The delicious tension that precedes release.

The glances between the two of them were growing more frequent and more electric and the black eyes seemed to follow her every movement. Amber felt a rush in the pit of her stomach. She just knew he was going to be a wonderful lover.

And now, finally, Abu Bakar and the others were standing up. Sheikh Zoltan stood up too and Amber did the same. Her heart raced as everyone began to bid each other goodnight, then nearly stopped as he came to stand beside her.

She felt his hand on her waist as he bent with a smile to say something. But as she glanced up at him, her senses spinning, suddenly he turned away, for at that moment a man came bursting into the tent, wild-eyed and frantic-looking, calling out his name.

As the man came rushing up to him, babbling something in Arabic, Amber watched, feeling a clutch of alarm in her heart. Then as Sheikh Zoltan's expression darkened, she noticed Saleh Ali hovering anxiously in the mouth of the tent and guessed instantly that there must be some bad news about the old man's grandson.

She was right. With a frown, Sheikh Zoltan turned to tell her, 'There's been some worrying news from London. The child's in a critical condition after his operation. I'm afraid I'm going to have to drive Saleh Ali into the city so he can spend the night by a phone.' Apologetically, he touched her arm. 'I'm sorry, *habibiti*. But I'm the only one who can take him.'

Just for a moment, the tears almost flew to Amber's eyes. It wasn't fair. Why did this have to happen now? But, in the very same instant, she felt a dart of shame for her selfishness. How could she think such things when there was a child seriously ill?

She looked up into his face. 'Then of course you must take him. And I hope there's better news waiting for you when you get there.'

'Let's hope there is.' Gently, he squeezed her arm. 'Thank you for understanding. I'll be back as soon as I can.'

Then, with a flurry of white robes, he hurried from the tent.

Amber walked back to her own tent in a daze of black misery. How could a day that had begun so full of promise have ended on such a wretched note as this? For quite apart from the tragic business of Saleh Ali's grandson, she felt as though her own world had suddenly fallen apart.

There was no chance that Zoltan would be able to get back to the camp tonight. Two hours' drive to the city. Two hours' drive back again. It would be the early hours of the morning at best before he returned. There'd be no night of love beneath the stars, after all.

She peeled off her beautiful dress, folded it carefully and lay on the bed, feeling totally bereft, close to weeping. Which was really quite ridiculous. Surely she was overreacting? It had been a horrible let-down, but it wasn't the end of the world. They could have their promised night of love tomorrow.

But telling herself that made her feel no better. The empty ache inside her just wouldn't go away. She lay staring at the tent roof. What's the matter with me? she puzzled. Surely I can't be that desperate to sleep with him? Surely I can manage to wait one more day?

She turned off the gas lamp and curled up in the darkness, pulling the thin cotton sheet over her shoulders. And it was as she lay there trying to concentrate on falling asleep that suddenly she understood what was at the root of her misery.

It wasn't just tonight. It was much more than that.

What was weighing on her was the knowledge that in a few days she'd be leaving. There was so little time left. That's why tonight was so precious.

Precious?

The word rang strangely in her head. Precious surely couldn't be what she really meant?

But as she repeated the word in her head again she realised it was. Precious was the only way to describe how she felt about each and every minute she spent with him.

Amber turned over onto her back and stared up into the blackness as understanding began to creep like a cold chill through her bones. He really did mean that much to her and it would kill her to leave this place, knowing, as she did, that she'd never be back. In a few days, when she said goodbye, it would be goodbye for ever.

She lay very still, feeling her heart throb inside her. Oh, God, she thought, I'm lost. I've gone and fallen in love with him.

'Don't bother getting up. I only came to look in on Maha.' Zoltan glanced from the startled-looking figure in the bed to the second bed alongside it where the little girl slept. 'I'm leaving now,' he said softly. 'You can go back to sleep.'

The woman was half-sitting up, pulling the covers around her, though she was wearing the sort of night-dress even a nun would have approved of.

'Where's the girl?' she demanded. 'The blonde English girl. She wasn't here today or yesterday. Has she gone away?' Her eyes were anxious dark pools in her face.

'No, she hasn't gone away. I thought I explained that. She'll be back here again tomorrow. There's no need to worry.'

The woman fixed him with a searching look. 'Maha was asking for her. She mustn't go away yet. The child still needs her.'

'I know the child still needs her. That's why she won't be leaving.' His eyes slid to the little girl, sleeping peacefully in her bed, one olive-skinned arm wrapped round a battered teddy bear. 'Surely you must know that no one in the world has the child's interests at heart more than I do?' He turned away impatiently. 'Now go back to sleep.'

But he was aware that the dark, troubled eyes stayed with him until he had finally left the room.

Zoltan had made the trip back to the city in double-quick time, speeding along the deserted highway as though the hounds of hell were after him—which was actually remarkably close to how he'd felt. If Amber was suffering over what had happened, he was suffering ten times as much. Frustration smouldered inside him like a slow-burning torch.

He had taken Saleh Ali back to the palace, where he would have a comfortable room and a phone at his disposal. Then he had waited while the old man called the private number at the London hospital and spoke to his son, who was standing by the phone.

The news, to their great relief. had been a great deal better than they'd feared. The little boy was still critical but his condition was now stable.

'Try not to worry,' Zoltan had told the old man, laying a concerned hand on his shoulder. 'Your grandson is in the hands of some of the best doctors in the world. Have faith in them. They'll do everything they possibly can to save him.'

'I know.' The old man had been desperately close to tears. 'And I, too, shall do everything I can for him. I shall pray.'

It had been Zoltan's intention, after leaving Saleh Ali, to look in quickly on Maha, then head back at speed to Amber. It was late, but perhaps not too late, and his whole body burned for her. This need to make love to her was like a demon in his blood.

And that was the trouble. That was the reason why, as he headed down the deserted corridors of the sleeping palace, he was making a conscious effort not to hurry. Demons were dangerous. They distorted your thinking. And his demons, in recent days, had definitely distorted his.

In the beginning, when he had first persuaded her to move into the palace, though he had desired her he had not really intended doing anything about it. That had quickly changed as his desire for her had grown. He would have her, he had decided, just as soon as he could.

But, now, when he was quite certain that she would put up no resistance—for he had seen that soft, melting look in her eyes tonight—he was suddenly feeling uneasy about these demons that possessed him.

He was behaving like some mad, impulsive adolescent and he had never behaved like that in his life before. What was he thinking of? Was he out of his mind to think of chasing across the desert after her at this time of night? She was only a woman—though an exceptionally lovely and special one. And, surely, no woman in the world was worth that?

Out in the courtyard, he climbed into the waiting blue Range Rover, headed out through the palace gates and on to the highway. He would drive back at normal speed, with a little more thought for his safety this time, and it didn't matter a damn that it would be after daybreak when he arrived. There would be plenty of other opportunities to make love to her. He would manage to survive without her tonight.

And he would show those demons that he could beat them, after all.

Amber stirred and opened her eyes. Something had disturbed her. A movement? A sound? She wasn't sure what. Drowsy with sleep, she peered into the darkness.

Now she heard it again. Heart beating, she half sat up. And at that precise moment the tent flap swung open.

At first it was difficult to make out anything at all. Just a dark silhouette against the moonlit sky. But she knew instantly who it was by the electricity that filled the air.

She held her breath and whispered softly, 'Zoltan? Is that you?'

There was a pause, then he answered.

'*Habibiti*, I have come.'

And as he stood for a moment, still holding the tent flap open, over his shoulder Amber could see a million twinkling stars.

CHAPTER TWELVE

AMBER awoke as the last stars were fading from the sky. She blinked her eyes open and lay very still, aware of a profound sense of total contentment. A feeling of being at peace with herself and with the world all around her, as though her spirit had found the home it had secretly been seeking.

She was lying with her cheek against Zoltan's shoulder, nestling in the warmth of the strong arm that embraced her, breathing in the scents of him, her heart beating with his. And she knew, with every single fibre of her being, that here was where she belonged and where she yearned to be always.

'You're awake.' As he spoke, he bent to kiss her face, his lips as sweet as melted honey. Then, as she glanced up to meet his eyes, he smiled. '*Sabah al-kheer.*'

A rush of happiness went through her as she looked into his face. '*Sabah al-kheer,*' she answered. She knew it meant good morning. It was one of the couple of phrases she'd learnt from Rashid.

Zoltan had turned over onto his side to gaze into her eyes. Amber gazed back, feeling a warm glow touch her heart. I love him, she kept thinking. I love him totally, without reservation. A sense of joy and fulfilment poured through her. It was as though she'd been waiting to love him all her life.

They were curled up together in her narrow trestle-bed, she in her pyjamas, he in the thin white trousers he always wore beneath his white robes. For they hadn't made love last night, after all. Instead, they'd simply lain wrapped in each other's arms, exchanging sleepy kisses before finally drifting off to sleep.

'Please understand,' he'd told her, 'that I want to make love to you. I want to make love to you more than anything in the world. But the night is almost over. Soon, the camp will be wakening. As much as I desire it, now would not be the right time. The first time I make love to you I want it to be special. I don't want it to be a rushed, hurried thing.'

He'd kissed her and held her. 'But I want to be with you. Let us sleep together the couple of hours that remain until dawn.'

Amber, in fact, had slept very little. To be truthful, she hadn't really wanted to sleep. What she'd wanted was to savour every precious moment at his side and to revel in the wonderful new sensations that filled her.

It hadn't mattered at all that there'd been no night of love. Maybe it was actually better that things had turned out like this and they'd been able to spend this quiet time together.

The whole thing had felt so right. As she'd lain there beside him, listening to his even, gentle breathing, the warmth of his naked torso pressed deliciously against her, she'd been aware of an easing of all the tension within her and of a peaceful sense of closeness with him that she'd felt with no man ever before.

At last, she understood him. There were no barriers any more. True, there were many things that still remained a mystery, but tonight it was as though a private window to his soul had miraculously been opened to her. Nothing about him would ever feel strange and alien again. And, as sudden light had seemed to flood the window of her own soul, she'd also understood that, as long as she lived, he was all she'd ever need or want to be happy.

She looked into his eyes now as he told her, 'It's time I left.' He stroked her cheek lightly and kissed her as he added, 'It's better that we don't risk anyone finding me here. No need to start tongues wagging in the camp.'

He paused and looked deep into her eyes for a long moment, making her feel as though her soul was melting inside her.

'We'll have tonight instead,' he promised. 'Back at the palace. Tonight I shall make love to you from the moment the first star appears until the last one finally fades from the sky.' He smiled and kissed her. 'How does that sound? Do I have your agreement to that plan?'

Amber nodded, feeling love and desire twist inside. 'Yes,' she answered huskily. 'You have my agreement.'

He stood up then and quickly began to get dressed, pulling on his white robe and his shoes and his white *kaffiyeh*. Amber watched him. He was so beautiful. Every move he made filled her with perfect, exquisite pleasure.

She felt a frisson deep inside her. An excited tightening in the pit of her stomach. Tonight, he would be hers. Tonight, when they made love.

She was still trying to catch her breath, her heart racing inside her, as he cast her one last smile and disappeared out through the tent flap.

'It has been a great pleasure meeting you. Any time you wish to return, we will be more than happy to welcome you back as our guest.'

'Thank you. You've been so kind. I'm really grateful for all your help.'

It was a couple of hours later and Amber and Zoltan were getting ready to leave the camp and return to the city. Amber was saying goodbye to Abu Bakar and the others. She turned to Nabila and gave the girl a warm hug.

'Thank you too,' she told her. '*Shokrun gazeelin*,' she added, airing another of the Arabic phrases she'd picked up and, in the process, saving Zoltan the trouble of translating.

Then, with a last wave to them all, she and Zoltan were heading for the car and climbing aboard to begin their journey back across the desert. They were alone together at last. A sense of magic filled the air, mingled with a thousand unspoken promises. Amber had never felt so happy or so excited in her life.

Glancing at her, Zoltan reached out to take hold of her hand and lay it, palm down, against his lightly clad thigh. 'Right,' he told her, 'for the next couple of hours I want you to tell me all about yourself. Your life story, from start to finish. All about your childhood and your family. I want to know every single thing about this beautiful woman who has so miraculously chanced into my life.'

The warm, muscular hardness of the flesh beneath her hand had sent a quick, hot flash of desire through Amber's loins. With an effort, she kept her hand still— for she longed to caress him, which might not be terribly wise while he was driving!—and answered, meeting his gaze, feeling her heart shift inside her at the mesmeric power of those wonderful black eyes,

'OK, but I'll tell you about me only for the first hour. For the second hour, you have to tell me all about you.'

Zoltan laughed. 'It's a deal.' He flicked her a smile. 'Right. I'm waiting. Start at the beginning. Where were you born?'

Amber sat back in her seat. 'I was born in Cambridge,' she told him. And for the next sixty minutes she went on to regale him with stories about the wonderful old family house she'd been brought up in, about her novelist mother and her Cambridge don father, her grandparents and aunts and uncles and cousins and the gloriously happy childhood she'd been blessed with.

She told him about her schooldays and the occasional scrapes she'd got into. 'When you have as curious a nature as I have,' she confessed, 'it sometimes gets you into trouble.'

Zoltan smiled at her. 'I'm extremely grateful that you have a curious nature,' he told her. 'Otherwise, you would never have come to Ras al-Houht. And your coming here was undoubtedly one of the best things that have ever happened to me.'

Amber lowered her gaze, feeling her heart skip as a flood of secret dreams and hopes went pouring through her. Had he really meant that? Did he care for her, if only a little? It was terrifying just how desperately she prayed that he did.

As she continued with her story, Zoltan listened with close attention, making frequent comments and asking lots of questions. 'What was the name of your pet Labrador?' 'Where did you live when you first moved to London?' But when she touched briefly on her love life all he said was, 'You really don't have to bother trying to convince me you're not fickle, you know. I didn't mean those things I said and, anyway, it doesn't matter.'

Amber felt oddly put down, for, of course, he'd guessed right. She did want him to know he'd been wrong in what he'd said. Aside from Adrian, there'd been only a handful of men in her life, and it was important to her that Zoltan should know this.

But what did he mean when he said it didn't matter? Was he trying to tell her that these things were of no interest to him? That their relationship was of too little significance for him to care?

Fear flooded through her. But then he turned quickly to smile at her, taking her hand in his and giving it a warm squeeze, and as she smiled back, her anguish instantly subsiding, she suddenly dared to wonder if what he'd actually been saying was that his feelings for her quite simply didn't require any such reassurance.

If only that were so. It was how she felt about him.

At last, her hour was up. 'Right. It's your turn now,' she told him. She sat back expectantly as he smiled and began to speak.

Zoltan's tale was every bit as fascinating as Amber had known it would be. The fifth child and first son of the old Emir and his only wife, he'd been brought up in the palace, surrounded by luxury and servants.

'From the age of four, however,' he told her, 'I had an English tutor called Arthur, who, as well as educating me and teaching me English, helped to introduce me to the big outside world. He did a lot to open my eyes— and the eyes of my three younger brothers as well.'

He cast her a wry smile. 'I've always been grateful for Arthur's influence. My father, though I loved him, was a man of narrow, traditional views, quite incapable of making the sorts of reforms the country was in need of. To give him his due, though, I've always suspected he was aware of this and that was why he employed Arthur in the first place—to give his sons what he, personally, was unable to give them. Namely, the necessary vision to bring the country into the end of the twentieth century.'

Amber listened, rapt, remembering how in the early days she'd doubted the motives behind all his reforms. Had it simply been an exercise in self-glorification? she'd wondered uncharitably.

Now she knew she'd been wrong. It had been nothing of the kind. When he spoke of the things he'd done and of his plans for the future, the passion and commitment in his voice were almost tangible. He cared about Ras al-Houht and about the welfare of its people. Knowing that, she felt deeply proud of him and loved him even more.

There was one area of his life, however, that was missing from the tale. So far, he'd said not a word about his love life. Naturally, she didn't expect him to go into details but, unlike him in this regard, she was definitely curious!

'So, why aren't you married?' she asked him with a frank smile. 'Surely, as the eldest son, and now as the Emir, it must be expected of you to marry and produce an heir? And, as you've told me, all of your eleven brothers and sisters are married.'

'I'll get round to it, too, before long, I've no doubt.'

As he finished the sentence, he glanced at her and smiled, but there was a strangely shuttered look at the back of his eyes. As though there was something he wasn't telling her, or had been about to say, but had changed his mind.

Some revelation about some woman in his past, perhaps? For there had to be someone. Perhaps even someone important. Foolishly, that last thought sent a stab of jealousy through Amber's heart.

But, whatever his secret was, he wasn't about to reveal it now. As they sped along the highway towards the palace, rapidly leaving the empty desert behind them, he was changing the subject and turning to tell her, 'When we arrive, I'll have to leave you to your own devices for a while. There are people I have to see, various matters I need to attend to.'

He reached for her hand and held it in his, then, twining his long, strong fingers with hers, let their two hands lie together in his lap.

'But, as soon as I can, I shall come to you,' he told her. And his eyes seemed to darken, his gaze pouring into hers, as he raised her hand slowly to kiss her fingertips softly. 'Just as soon as the first star appears in the sky.' He cast a smouldering glance across at her. 'So, be ready for me,' he warned.

Amber looked back at him, feeling her heart swell with longing inside her. With longing, with love and with the surest conviction that these moments she was living were the most precious of her life.

She leaned across and quickly touched her lips to his cheek.

'Don't worry,' she told him. 'I'll be ready.'

Less than eight hours had passed, but the dragging day had seemed endless.

Amber had busied herself out in the courtyard,

transcribing interviews from her tape recorder and making notes for the few interviews that still remained to be done. But not even for a single second had she managed to douse the thought that burned constantly at the back of her mind.

Zoltan.

Her brain whirred and her body burned in anticipation.

And now the time had almost come.

She was sitting in a cane chair in the moonlit courtyard, newly bathed and scented and dressed in a kaftan of palest turquoise, her stomach twisted into a million tight little knots as she watched the peacock pecking amongst the cobblestones and tried to keep herself from glancing up every five seconds to search the sky anxiously for stars.

What if he didn't come? After last night, he might be tired. She pushed the thought from her. If he doesn't come, I shall die.

She kept her eyes fixed on the peacock. Tell him to hurry. Tell him I need him. Tell him I can't wait any longer.

The peacock carried on pecking, fluttered its tail feathers and said nothing.

But then, a sudden movement in the doorway behind her. Her heart leapt, but, before she had time to turn round, two hands had come to rest lightly on her shoulders and a pair of warm lips was brushing the back of her neck. Simultaneously, all in one breath, Amber started and shuddered, leaning back as his hands slid down to cup her breasts.

His lips moved round to her mouth. 'Once again, I

didn't knock. No manners, you see,' he teased her.
'And, anyway, I wanted to surprise you.'

He was drawing her from the chair, coming round to
stand before her, then ever so gently taking her face in
his hands and bending to press his lips against hers. At
the warm, erotic touch of him, a fire flickered in her
loins.

'I didn't realise the first star had risen in the sky yet,'
she answered huskily.

'It will soon. I couldn't wait.' He swept her up into his
arms, effortlessly, as though she weighed no more than
a feather. Then he was carrying her into the bedroom
and laying her on the bed amongst the pillows. He
kissed her. 'I couldn't wait another single minute.'

As he spoke, he was already shedding his clothes,
dropping them without caring where they landed, to
stand before her, at last, naked and hungry.

And he was indeed beautiful. As she looked at him,
Amber shivered. Every inch of him was glorious, virile
perfection. Smooth, hard muscle. Lean, powerful limbs.
She remembered her dream. Well, the reality was even
better.

And now he was bending to slip her kaftan over her
head and slide away the panties which were all she was
wearing underneath. He sat down on the edge of the
bed to gaze at her for a moment as she lay there quite
unselfconsciously exposed in her nakedness. With his
two hands he caressed her—her breasts, her flanks, her
thighs—making her shiver deliciously and catch her
breath.

'How beautiful you are. Even more beautiful than I
had imagined.' He bent quickly to kiss the soft triangle
of golden hair. Then he raised his eyes to look at her

again. 'I'd better warn you,' he told her, 'that I plan to get to know every single centimetre of this beautiful body.'

He nuzzled his lips against her breast. 'I hope you're ready for me,' he breathed.

With gentle expertise, his hands poured over her, his fingers caressing, teasing, arousing. Amber felt herself go limp and taut with desire at the same time. A fire was rushing through her. Sparks were flying from her skin.

Reaching out for him, she buried her face against his chest and hungrily entwined her long, slim legs with his. And, as his manhood pressed against her, her insides turned to liquid. She'd never been more ready for anything in her life.

He must have sensed the urgency within her, and Amber could feel the throbbing urgency in him. But he did not hurry. Wickedly, he took his time.

'You are almost ready,' he told her, 'but not quite ready enough.'

Gently, he turned her over onto her front; then, sitting astride her, lightly pinning her down, he began to massage her with firm, cool strokes. Her shoulders, her neck, her back, her arms.

'You are too tense,' he told her, his hands sweeping over her. 'Every muscle in your entire body must be loose and relaxed.'

Amber felt as though she was disintegrating, as though she must melt into the bed. Every stroke of his hands was stoking the fire within her. She was being consumed by a seething, raging furnace.

At last, he flipped her over on to her back again, his hands swift and gentle as they loosened the bunched-up muscles of her neck, her shoulders, her arms, her wrists.

A feeling of lightness began to flow through her. It was a wonderful sensation. Almost like floating.

But the more relaxed she became, the more fiercely her need burned. It flowed through her like a bubbling red-hot stream of lava. Any minute now she'd go up in a shower of sparks.

I'm ready! Please! I'm ready! she implored silently with her eyes, though really she felt like yelling it at the top of her lungs.

Couldn't he see that, at this rate, there'd be nothing left of her soon?

Zoltan was well aware of the hungry heat that burned in her. And she was almost ready now for this moment he had dreamed of and that would only be spoiled if they were to hurry it. It was a moment to be savoured with all one's senses and without haste.

He had been wise, he reflected, to deny himself last night. The time had not been right. It would have been a mistake. The demons that, after all, had sent him hurrying back to her, in spite of his resolution to fight them, at least had failed to impair his judgement totally.

With a sigh, he bent down and kissed her on the lips, feeling the shiver that raced through her, feeling a shiver within himself. And now, as his hands swept over her naked body, his touch had magically transformed into a caress.

His hands cupped her breasts, the most beautiful breasts in all the world, firm and full, the dark nipples as hard as iron as he strummed them with the flat of his thumbs. He bent down and took one of them firmly in his mouth.

She let out a soft whimper, her body arching against

him, and he could feel her limbs tremble as he swept one hand down to caress the silky-soft flesh of her inner thighs. He had always known that making love to her would be exciting. He had sensed her responsiveness, the secret fire that burned within her. And he could feel it scorch him now, like a naked flame against his skin.

As he kissed her again, she was reaching out to caress him, her fingers like torches against his brightly aware skin. He felt a clench, like a steel trap springing inside him. 'Now,' he whispered hoarsely. 'Now you are ready.'

Her arms twined round his neck as he slid down on top of her. and he could feel her thighs part beneath him in welcome. Then he was holding her fast, meeting her hungry mouth with his, and it was impossible to tell as he thrust inside her whether it was his own cry of joy or hers that filled his ears.

CHAPTER THIRTEEN

'So, TELL me, have you decided yet to stay?'

It was three in the afternoon the following day and they were lying together in a tangle of naked limbs amongst the tumbled lace pillows of the big white bed. Zoltan had one arm around Amber's shoulders, the fingers of his free hand lacing with hers, while Amber lay against him, her head resting against his chest. She felt happier than she'd ever believed it possible to be.

As he spoke, Zoltan bent to kiss her on the cheek. 'Tell me you're not planning to go back to England straight away.'

Amber turned to meet his eyes, her heart shifting with helpless love for him, just as it did every single time she looked at him. And, as always, the strength of her feelings surprised her. Where had all this love in her come from when it hadn't been there before?

'I've got to stay for a day or two,' she told him in a teasing tone. She smiled and kissed him. 'I still have some interviews to do.'

Zoltan growled and bit her ear, his arm tightening around her. 'So, you would torment me, would you?' He gave her a playful squeeze. 'Heartless woman, you know very well what I'm talking about. I want to know what's going to happen when all your interviews are done.'

He kissed her. 'As I keep telling you, I want you to

stay. Say you will. You know in your heart it's what you want too.'

Amber looked back at him. Yes, it *was* what she wanted. But, just like all the other times before when he'd asked her, something was stopping her from saying that she'd stay.

It was all so strange and so sudden. It would be a huge step to take. Her entire life would suddenly be turned on its head. Though that prospect didn't scare her. She wanted to change her life now. From now on, she longed for her life to be with Zoltan. Perhaps she hesitated simply because she needed to catch her breath.

She told him, being practical, 'Even if I did decide to stay, you know I have to be back in London at the end of the week.' She'd explained about Don and his California trip. 'And, anyway, I have a business I can't just turn my back on.'

'I know, but we can always find a way round that problem. The important thing is that you decide to make your life here with me.' Zoltan hugged her. 'But, don't worry. I'm not trying to rush you.' He raised her fingers to his lips and grazed her knuckles with a kiss, sending a flurry of electric little shivers rushing through her. 'Think about it over the next couple of days. You don't have to decide now. I know it's a big decision.'

Then he paused, his expression suddenly growing fierce as he looked at her, his arm tightening round her shoulders as he growled a warning. 'Only, be very, very certain that you make the right decision! Take my word for it, *habibiti*, I have no intention of letting you go.'

'You mean you'll make me a prisoner, after all?' Amber joked. 'You mean you'll lock me up, just as I thought you planned to do in the beginning?'

A look flickered across his eyes. 'Maybe I will,' he told her darkly. 'If that's what it takes to make you stay.'

Amber knew he wasn't serious. She looked back at him with a smile, feeling far more flattered by than afraid of his threat. As yet, like herself, he hadn't spoken the word 'love'. Perhaps, also like her, he felt a little awed by such strong feelings. But she could sense the emotion in him, like a heat that embraced her. And she recognised it because it was the same powerful heat that flowed through her.

There was something else he hadn't spoken about—what would she be if she stayed? Was she simply to be his lover? Or would he want her to be his wife? If she were to remain, it was essential that the answer be the latter.

But he would know that and, surely, it would be the same for him? The man she'd come to know wouldn't be asking her to stay unless he'd decided his intentions were serious.

She smiled to herself. It was a little hard to take in the momentous chain of events over the past forty hours or so that had contrived to change the world for ever.

The revelation that she was in love with him. His coming to her tent. Those few precious hours they'd lain chastely together. Then, last night, making love, again and again, till the last star had finally faded from the sky and, exhausted and content, they'd fallen asleep in each other's arms.

And now this latest and least expected development of all. His asking her to stay and make her life here with him.

'*Habibiti. . .*'

He was kissing her and drawing her into his arms. As

he pressed against her, Amber could feel the desire in him stirring—and an instant answering stirring within herself.

She rolled on top of him and kissed him, gazing down at his adored face, melting into the dark eyes, drowning in her need for him. A moment ago, he'd joked about making her his prisoner, but, if he only knew it, she was his prisoner already. Bound to him for ever, with no hope of escape.

For what stronger chains exist than the invisible chains of love?

The next couple of days passed in a haze of blissful happiness.

Amber was busy for much of the time doing the rest of her interviews and Zoltan was kept occupied with various affairs of state. But, even when they were apart, Amber felt as though he was with her. And when they were together it couldn't have been more perfect.

It was so easy to be with him. She seemed to have known him all her life. Even the new things she kept discovering about him—like his love of Mozart and classical painting, and the tiny scar from a childhood fall he had under his chin—felt instantly familiar, as though some part of her had already known them. It was hard to believe they hadn't been together for years, imposs- ible to credit it had only been just over a week.

They ate together whenever they could and slept side by side in the big white bed, and on their second night together Zoltan finally kept his promise to explain to her all the secrets of the vast Arabian sky.

Sometimes, he'd join her out in the courtyard for an hour as she sat studying the archives or transcribing some interviews. And it was on one of these visits that he gave her the good news about Saleh Ali's little grandson.

'The crisis is over. We just got the news from London. The doctors say he'll be able to come home in about a week.'

Amber was delighted. 'I'll bet the old man's over the moon!'

As she said it, she thought about her own piece of news which, at least in the meantime, she was keeping to herself. For, just about an hour ago, she'd received a fax from Don informing her that his trip to California had been postponed and that there was no longer any need for her to go rushing back.

I'll tell Zoltan, she'd decided, once I've made up my mind whether or not I really want to stay. For she still wasn't certain and he'd only start pressuring her if he knew.

Amber had pondered pretty well endlessly on her reluctance to take the plunge, and she'd come to the conclusion that what was holding her back wasn't just the fact that everything had happened so fast. Nor was it because she was unsure of her feelings for Zoltan. On that score, there wasn't a shred of doubt in her mind. It was impossible to imagine loving any other man.

But there were still some things that troubled her, the most important of which was the feeling she sometimes had that he was keeping something from her. Something important. Something she ought to know. Then there was the business about the library and his attitude to women, which just didn't seem to fit with the man she'd grown to love.

That worried her. Did she really know him as well as she thought?

It was on the second afternoon, when he came to join her out in the courtyard, that Amber took the opportunity to try and resolve at least one mystery.

'You know,' she told him as he popped one of her favourite *halwa* into her mouth—for he always arrived with some treat to surprise her, like a dish of little almond cakes or a bunch of fresh flowers—'I still sometimes feel as though I'm being watched while I'm sitting here. Just a moment before you arrived, in fact, I was sure someone was there.'

As she spoke, she glanced up at the half-shuttered window above the French window. 'Sometimes, I even feel as though there's more than one person.'

Zoltan frowned as he looked her. 'Does it bother you very much? I mean, does it put you off your work?' he wanted to know.

'Not really.' Amber shook her head. 'I try just to ignore it.' She looked deep into the black eyes. 'But it does make me curious. It's that woman again, isn't it? Why does she keep watching me?' She frowned. 'And why won't you tell me who she is?'

'I've told you who she is. I told you she's a servant.' He paused, his gaze flickering uncomfortably for a moment. But the look vanished instantly as he leaned towards her, taking her hands in his and telling her in an earnest tone, 'There's no harm in her. Don't worry. Just try to ignore her. I promise you there really is nothing to be concerned about.'

'I know that. I'm not afraid of her. I just want to understand what's going on.' She frowned into his face.

'There must be some reason why she keeps watching me. Why won't you tell me? Why is it such a secret?'

There was a little more emotion in her voice than she'd intended. All the feelings she'd been holding back—the frustration and confusion—were suddenly laid bare and out in the open.

'I don't understand it and, what's more, I don't like it,' she added.

Zoltan reacted instantly. With a frown of concern, he drew her into his arms and held her close for a moment.

'*Habibiti*, I would never do anything to upset you. How can you even think such a thing? Surely you know me better? Don't you know how much you mean to me?'

As she blinked at him, a little surprised at the naked anguish in his voice, he continued, 'Believe me, I have no wish to keep secrets from you, but there are things, situations, that you cannot understand yet.'

He looked deep into her eyes. 'Be patient and trust me. I promise I'll explain everything to you just as soon as the time is right.'

'Why can't you explain now?'

'I'll explain soon. I promise.' He kissed her. 'Now tell me that you trust me,' he demanded, 'and that you will never think such angry thoughts again.'

Amber was totally won over. 'Very well,' she consented. 'As long as you promise to tell me soon.'

'Very soon.'

She smiled. 'And of course I trust you,' she told him.

And she did. Absolutely. Without any reservation. Which was why, a little later, after he'd gone to attend a meeting, Amber finally made up her mind.

I'm going to stay, she decided. I'm going to take a

chance. I'm going to follow my instincts and listen to my heart. And, besides, it was pointless delaying the decision any longer. She was fooling herself by pretending to be uncertain. Wild horses wouldn't have dragged her back to England.

She felt like rushing to tell him, but he wouldn't be out of his meeting yet. He'd warned her it would probably drag on for a couple of hours. Still, in the meantime, there were one or two useful things she could do.

The first was to call the airport and cancel her reservation. The second was to get off a fax to her mother to let her know she'd decided to stay on for a while and that she'd fax her an outline of all the research she'd done. After she'd spoken to Zoltan, she'd phone her and explain what was going on!

These two modest chores took less than fifteen minutes. Restlessly, she began to pace about the room. It was pointless trying to work. She'd never be able to concentrate. Tired of pacing, she went outside and spoke to the peacock for a bit, then sat down at her table and flicked distractedly through some notes. Back inside, she prowled aimlessly about the bedroom for a while, then she washed her hair and took a shower, and, finally, after having glanced at her watch at least a thousand times, two hours had gone by—the longest two hours of her entire life.

She slipped on her prettiest dress, a simple shift in shades of blue, sprayed herself rather more lavishly than usual with scent and headed excitedly for the library. For he'd be in his office. She was pretty sure of that. Over the past couple of days, she'd learned a lot about his routine. And the quickest way to his office was through the library.

It was as she was hurrying past the row of private study cubicles which Zoltan had pointed out to her when he'd shown her round that time that something inadvertently caught her eye. But though it struck her as strange she didn't pause to think about it. In fact, it barely registered at all. There was only one thing on her mind. Telling Zoltan her good news!

She made her way through the archives room and stepped out into a corridor, at the end of which, if she'd got her geography right, ought to be his offices. Her heart was dancing in her chest as she imagined the look on his face when she walked through the door and made her announcement.

As she neared the end of the corridor, she could see quite clearly the big gold sign in Arabic and English announcing that behind the panelled wood door lay the office of Sheikh Zoltan bin Hamad al-Khalifa, Emir of the Princely State of Ras al-Houht.

She smiled. Could this really be the same man she loved? The man whom she thought of simply as Zoltan these days, whose heart and body and soul she knew so well and to whom she was about to commit her future?

The door was slightly ajar. She stepped towards it, eyes bright with excitement, her lips formed to say his name. But, as she pushed the door open, the light in her eyes died. All at once, she couldn't speak. It was as though she'd turned to stone.

He was standing by the window beside the very large teak desk that dominated the enormous bookcase-lined room. He had his back half-turned towards her and he wasn't alone.

In his arms he held a child, an extremely pretty little girl. Amber guessed she was probably four or five years old. And at his side stood a woman, dressed from head to toe in black, though she was wearing her *chador* drawn back from her face. She was quite beautiful, perhaps a year or so older than herself, and though this was the first time she'd ever seen her face Amber knew instantly who she was.

She was the woman who'd been following her and spying on her from the window. The woman she'd almost bumped into outside the courtyard door that time. The woman she'd once suspected might be Zoltan's jealous wife.

With a plummeting feeling of despair, she knew now that she'd been right. For it didn't take a great deal of intelligence to work out that what she was looking at was a cosy family scene. Zoltan was talking to the child in Arabic, the child smiling in response, while the woman stood watching them with a tender, indulgent smile.

It was the woman who spotted Amber first. Suddenly, she turned, panic darting in her eyes. Amber heard her catch her breath and let out a startled gasp.

Less than an instant later, Zoltan was turning too, though Amber didn't wait to see the expression on his face.

'Liar!' she screamed at him. 'Liar! Liar! Liar!' Then she was turning on her heel and fleeing out the door.

She heard him shout, 'Come back!' but she paid no attention, just flew down the corridor as fast as her legs would carry her, feeling as though she was tumbling through the fiery gates of hell.

Her heart was splintering inside her, her lungs bursting in her chest. No wonder he'd never mentioned marriage. He was married already. Married with a child.

And as for love? That was a joke. It was quite plain that he'd never loved her. If he'd loved her, he could never have deceived her like this.

He'd just used her. That was all. That was the cruel, ugly truth.

As she hurtled down the maze of corridors back to her room, Amber felt as though her brain was exploding in her head. It was over. Just like that. Her dreams in ashes at her feet. Her brief moment of happiness brutally exposed for the empty, self-deluding fantasy it had been. She'd just been taken for the most cynical ride of her life.

All he'd ever wanted was a tawdry affair. He'd only asked her to stay so she could be his handy, live-in sex toy. And perhaps, after all, she'd been right in the beginning when she'd wondered if that was why he'd brought her here in the first place.

At last she'd reached her room. She burst through the door, sobbing. Well, that would never be. She'd never be his toy. Blind with tears, she slammed the door shut, fell against it and turned the key, then she rushed over to the French window and locked that as well. This room was her fortress. He'd never lay a hand on her again. She'd die before she'd allow him to set even one foot across the threshold!

As she stood in the middle of the room, breathing hard, fighting her anguish, suddenly the fax machine in the corner started to chatter. Automatically, she went over and snatched the message that had come through, seeing at once that it was from her mother.

'Congratulations!' it said. 'He must be a very special

man! Phone soon, darling. Your father and I are dying to hear all about him. In the meantime, just enjoy yourself and be happy.'

Amber read the cheerful message and felt her heart turn to dust. Trust her mother, with her incurably romantic turn of mind, to guess there was a man at the root of her decision to stay on, but how totally, sadly wrong she was when she said he must be special. There was nothing special about him. He was a lying, cheating snake!

She stared down miserably at the fax, hot tears pricking at her eyes as the words 'be happy' seemed to jump off the page to mock her. That was too cruel. She crushed the message into a ball and dropped it into the bin by her feet. She'd never be happy again as long as she lived.

As a tear rolled down her cheek, there was a sudden sound behind her. Startled, Amber swung round, her heart thudding against her ribs.

Then she froze.

Surely she was seeing things? It just wasn't possible. Zoltan was sitting in the armchair at the side of the bed.

'At last, I have your attention.' He rose to his feet with a dark smile. 'Now kindly listen to what I have to say to you. I think it's time we finally got a few things straight.'

CHAPTER FOURTEEN

'How did you get in here?' Amber stared at Zoltan in disbelief, her sense of shock for the moment obscuring every other emotion. 'What the devil's going on? I've just locked the door and window!' She glanced round her as though to make sure she wasn't dreaming.

Zoltan had come to stand before her, his expression a little lighter now. 'Don't worry,' he told her. 'There's really no mystery. I got here before you. You didn't see me when you walked in.'

That was certainly possible. She'd been blind with misery and tears. 'But how could you have got here before me?' That was the weird bit. 'I ran all the way.'

He smiled. 'I obviously ran faster. And I know a couple of shortcuts.'

'Ah.' Amber dropped her gaze. That smile had scraped a tender nerve. In the past, his quick smile had always filled her with such pleasure. Now it was just a bitter reminder of everything she'd lost.

Impatiently, she turned away, brushing the wetness from her cheeks. He was a rat, not worth a single one of her tears, and she was a fool to let him see them.

She said in a rough tone, 'Well, you could have saved yourself the trouble. I don't want to hear whatever it is you've come to say and I'd actually be rather grateful if you'd just leave.'

Zoltan looked at her for a moment through narrowed dark eyes, then, by way of a response to her angry invitation, he laid his hands on her shoulders and, holding her firmly, began to guide her towards the bed.

Amber stiffened and tried to resist. 'Let me go! What do you think you're doing?' Remembering her recent thoughts about the fate he had in store for her, she wondered if she ought to be afraid.

But as she looked into his face there was no fear in her heart at all, just a sense of desolation, as vast as the desert, that this man she loved so desperately would never be hers.

'Sit down,' he told her. 'Sit down and listen to what I have to say.'

'Listen to more lies, you mean?' Anger helped to soothe the pain. As she seated herself on the edge of the bed, Amber's eyes flashed up at him like knives. 'I really don't know why you're insisting,' she protested. 'There's not a snowball's chance in hell of me believing anything you tell me.'

'If you say so. But I plan to tell you anyway.'

He stepped away from her and went to stand by one of the small tables, on the same spot where he'd stood during one of their early confrontations, when he'd taken a rose from the vase and bent to breathe its scent. Amber remembered all this with a tug of despair and quickly lowered her eyes to the tiled floor.

He was continuing, 'None of this would be necessary if you'd trusted me enough to believe what I've already told you. I told you I wasn't married and that is the truth. Selma, the woman you saw me with a few minutes ago, is a servant—something else I've already told you. She happens to be the little girl's nanny.'

'Nanny?' A wave of relief poured through her. 'Oh,

Zoltan! Forgive me! I jumped to completely the wrong conclusion.'

Her face broke into a smile. He hadn't lied to her, after all. She started to get up, to go to him, to embrace him, but with an unexpectedly cool look he signalled to her to sit down again.

'Wait,' he told her with an edge of sharpness. 'I haven't finished yet.'

Amber reseated herself, chastened. What was coming next?

She had a sudden intuition. 'And the child? Is she yours?'

'No, she is not mine. But it is about the child that I must now explain—as I was already planning to do anyway very soon.' Zoltan took a deep breath and paced the floor for a moment. 'Her name is Maha. She is the child of my dead sister. Both my sister and her husband were killed in an accident just over a year ago. Since then, I have been the child's guardian and, to the best of my ability, also her father. Selma, in truth, has been more than just a nanny. She has been the next best thing to a mother.'

As he'd spoken, his face had changed. Though a shadow had briefly fallen when he'd mentioned the death of his sister and her husband, it had vanished the instant he'd returned to the subject of the child. In its place, a look of love had flooded his features.

At such honest emotion Amber's heart had squeezed inside her. It was perfectly obvious that he adored the little girl.

Then he surprised her. He turned to look at her, a frown darkening his face again. 'It is because of the child that I brought you here,' he said.

'Because of the child?'

Without quite knowing why, Amber felt a sudden anxious chill touch her skin. She was aware that she was holding her breath as he continued, 'At first, after the initial trauma, she seemed to accept the loss of her parents. She is young, after all, and the young heal quickly. But about six months ago her behaviour began to change. . .'

As he spoke, he continued to pace the floor and not once did he even so much as glance in her direction.

'She became withdrawn, refusing to go out or to speak to anyone but me or Selma. We tried to coax her out of it, but it simply got worse. In the end, we couldn't even persuade her to leave her room. She wouldn't eat. She was wasting away. I was almost at my wits' end.'

Even now, Amber could hear the desperation in his voice. 'So, what did you do?' she asked him quietly.

'I called in the experts. Psychologists. Psychiatrists. Therapists. Trauma counsellors. Every kind of expert I could find. . .'

'And what did they say?'

'Various things. All sorts of different therapies and counselling were tried, but none of them made any lasting difference. In spite of all their efforts, she just continued to get worse.'

He paused and sighed. Then he took a deep breath and, standing with his back half-turned to her, continued, 'But then, a couple of months ago, she started having these dreams. . . Dreams about a blonde-haired angel who came to save her. She began to speak about her all the time. It became a kind of obsession. And in the end I grew convinced that the only way to save her was for me to somehow find this angel. . .'

As he swung round to face her, Amber knew what he was about to say next. She waited to be proved right, feeling her skin turn to ice.

His eyes blazed as he looked at her. 'You probably think me crazy, but one day on my way back from a hunting trip with Rashid I saw you through my field-glasses and instantly knew that you were the angel who could save Maha's life.'

Amber could scarcely breathe. Every inch of her was trembling. 'And that was the real reason you invited me to the palace and why you were so anxious for me to stay.'

It was a statement not a question. There wasn't really any doubt. With a shaft of helpless pain, she was suddenly remembering how he'd told her, on their drive back from the Bedouin camp together, that her arrival in Ras al-Houht was one of the best things that had ever happened to him. At the time, she'd dared to hope that what he was really saying was that he cared for her, but now she knew the truth and she felt numb to her soul.

So. I was right. I mean nothing to him. He's just used me, after all.

Zoltan had turned away again and now he was continuing with his story.

'I installed you in the room with the private little courtyard because Maha's playroom overlooks the courtyard. And that was also why I had the table set up for you there—so you would spend as much time in the courtyard as possible.'

He cast a glance at her over his shoulder. 'The eyes you felt watching you were Maha's and Selma's. And it was Selma who locked the door of your room that first day—though she unlocked it again when she heard me coming down the corridor. She did it because she was terrified you might try to leave—the same reason that prompted her into following you around.

'Rashid, too,' he added, 'had the same fear. That was why he kept such a close eye on you that first time you went to town.'

He sighed and shook his head. 'So much depended on your staying. I think all of us would have done virtually anything to make you stay.'

Amber could feel a nervous pulse beating like a hammer in her head. This story he was telling her was a tale of pure horror. From start to finish, she'd been manipulated and used.

How could he have treated her like this, as though she were some kind of non-person? For that was what he'd done. All she'd been to him was a tool. Nothing more than a handy solution to a problem. She felt utterly paralysed with humiliation and grief.

She looked at him. 'Thank you for explaining everything to me so nicely. At last I understand what's been going on.' Her tone was glacial. As hard as rock. 'I'm so glad I was able to be of use,' she added.

'Amber!' He swung round with a pained look to face her. 'Amber, I realise how it must seem to you. But I had no choice. I had to do it. . .'

'Why didn't you just tell me? If you'd told me, I'd have helped you.' As she looked at him, the tears were suddenly clawing at her throat. 'If I'd known that the welfare of a child depended on it, I'd have moved into the palace without a second thought. I'd have sat out in the courtyard all day if you'd wanted me to. . .'

Her voice was cracking as she continued, all her hurt pouring out now. 'There was no need for you to go to the trouble of all that subterfuge. I'd have helped you anyway. All you had to do was ask—' She stumbled on a sob, unable to say more.

'Amber, how could I have asked you? You would have thought me insane. Anyone would have thought that. I know I felt insane. If I'd asked, you would never have agreed to go along with me and, try to understand, I just couldn't take that risk.'

'I do understand. But you're wrong. I *would* have helped. You ought to have asked me. You ought at least to have tried.'

'Maybe you're right. Maybe I should have. Maybe you're the one in a thousand who would have helped.' He sighed. 'But I didn't know you then. I didn't know how kind you are.'

He came and stood before her and she could sense his distress. 'Believe me, Amber, I only did what I thought best. I was out of my mind with worry and it was the only solution I could see. This angel thing had become an obsession with me too, and when I saw you I knew you were the answer to my prayers. So I had to do it. I just couldn't take the risk of letting Maha's only hope slip away.'

As he reached down and took her hands, which were clenched like steel traps in her lap, Amber looked into his face and knew he was speaking the truth. He really had believed there was no other way to save the child. And perhaps, if she'd been in his shoes, she'd have felt the same.

'OK,' she said. 'Maybe you did have no choice.'

After all, she reasoned, he'd done her no harm. On the contrary, he'd given her invaluable help with her work. In the end, it had probably been a fair enough exchange.

So she could forgive him for that. But not for the rest. She couldn't forgive him for the way he'd seduced her—as a cynical ploy to persuade her to stay. Surely she deserved just a little more respect?

She stood up to face him, roughly freeing her hands from his, fighting to hold onto her composure. 'So, now what? How is the little girl? Do you need me to stay on a little longer? I'm quite prepared to do that, as I've already told you.' It didn't need saying that that was *all* she was prepared to do.

Zoltan was watching her. He smiled a wry smile. 'I thought it might be necessary for you to stay on a bit longer, but, since today, I don't believe it will be, after all. She's made enormous progress over the past couple of days. She's eating again, speaking to everyone and perfectly happy to leave her room. In fact, she's almost back to being the child she used to be.'

His eyes filled with relief and joy and gratitude. 'And I have you to thank for that. It was you who worked the miracle.'

The soft look in his eyes was like a knife against Amber's heart. He was capable of such deep love, but, alas, not for her.

'I'm glad,' she said, fighting the sudden storm inside her. 'In that case, I'll arrange to catch the first plane back to London. I take it you have no objections?'

When he said nothing, she stepped past him. 'Good,' she observed coldly. She headed for the French doors. Suddenly, she had to escape. The tension inside her was making it hard to breathe. 'And now, if you don't mind, I need some fresh air.'

She laid her hand on the handle, then remembered the doors were locked, twisted the key, her fingers feeling like putty, and finally, impatiently pulled the doors open. Beyond the courtyard lay the gardens. A nice long walk might clear her head. Then she'd come back and phone the airport and book herself on the first available flight and just pray that she would never have to set eyes on him again.

Zoltan watched as she turned the key and pulled the doors open, a thousand and one thoughts flying through his head, though there was only one that really mattered.

She's walking out of my life. I'm going to lose her for ever. It was shocking how profoundly that prospect appalled him. How would he ever manage without her now?

He felt something wrench inside him as she began to step through the doorway. It was as though his body and his soul were parting company. You're crazy, he told himself. What are you waiting for? You know what you want to do. For heaven's sake, go ahead and do it!

He opened his mouth. He heard himself say, 'Before you go, there's just one thing I'd like to ask you.'

She was turning to look at him, anger in her face, as though she resented this delay, just wanted to be gone. Her tone was cold and harsh as she told him, 'I hope you're not thinking of asking me to stay. I can assure you right now there's no chance of that.'

It was like a slap in the face. He looked back at her and shook his head. 'No,' he told her, 'that was not the question.' He took a step towards her. 'What I want to ask is this. . .'

As he paused, he reflected that he'd thought this would be difficult, but, now that he'd started, it wasn't difficult at all. It was the easiest, most natural thing in the world. Yet he'd fought so hard against it, with all that nonsense about demons. And, once before, when he'd been tempted to make a similar move—that time when she'd asked him why he wasn't married with an heir—he'd told himself he was mad even to be considering such a thing.

That seemed impossible now. How could he have been so blind? Why had it taken him so long to face the fact that, without her, his life would be nothing?

But, perhaps, even now, it wasn't too late.

She was still watching him, waiting. His gaze poured over her face. That adored blue-eyed face that meant virtually the whole world to him.

Then he took a deep breath.

'Amber will you marry me?'

'You lied to me, you know. Don't try to deny it. I happen to have seen the evidence with my own eyes.'

They were lying together on the huge silk divan that stood in one corner of Zoltan's private sitting room, a tray of sweetmeats balanced on the cushions at their feet, a soft breeze wafting over them from the open window.

Three hours had passed since that shock proposal, to which Amber's sole response at first had been sheer amazement. Knocked totally speechless, she'd stood in the doorway blinking. Then she'd managed to croak, 'What did you say?'

He'd come to stand in front of her. 'I said I want to marry you.' His eyes were filled with fierce emotion.

'Believe me, I have never wanted anything so much in my life.'

Amber continued to blink at him as he took her hands in his. How could this be? The world had gone crazy. Just a moment ago she'd been about to walk out on him, determined to turn her back on him for ever, convinced that he'd used her that he cared nothing for her at all. And now this? It made no sense. She looked back at him, her brain spinning.

He raised her hands to his lips and kissed her fingers one by one, the dark eyes never leaving hers for a single moment. 'Will you, Amber? Will you be my wife?' His voice was full of gentle, urgent pleading. 'I love you. If you care for me at all, please say yes.'

Her sense of shock was starting to pass. The spinning in her head was slowing down. Amber opened her mouth, took a deep breath and said, 'Yes.'

It was as though a thousand Roman candles had suddenly gone off in the room. He took hold of her and hugged her and kissed her with such passion that she found herself laughing out loud in sheer delight. And in that moment she knew that, whatever lay before them, she'd spend the rest of her life blessing the decision she'd just made.

A little while later, Zoltan took her to meet Maha.

'She was the one who brought us together,' he said. 'She ought to be the first to hear the news.'

Amber instantly liked the bright-eyed little girl and laughed when, via their mutual interpreter, Maha told her, 'I used to think you were an angel, but even though I know you're not now I still think you're pretty.'

'I think you're pretty too.' Amber ruffled the dark

hair. 'And I just know we're going to be the very best of friends.'

Zoltan also introduced her to Selma—who finally felt able to look her straight in the eye!

'She says she wants to apologise if she scared you,' Zoltan translated, 'and that she would very much like to be friends with you too.'

'Tell her I'm sure we will be.' Amber smiled at the young woman, who, now that she was relaxed and smiling, wasn't sinister in the least. In fact, she had a lovely, sensitive, caring face.

It was also perfectly clear that she had an excellent relationship with her employer.

As Zoltan told Amber, 'I'm very fond of Selma. We fell out after she locked you in your room and started following you around, because I knew that sort of thing would only frighten you away. But she didn't mean any harm. She's a good woman at heart.'

After bidding a temporary farewell to Maha and Selma, Zoltan took her, for the very first time, to his private quarters, which were much less grand, though every bit as exquisite, as Amber had expected.

'Grandness is fine for the public rooms,' he told her, 'but I like my private space to be a bit more intimate. This, after all, is where I come to relax.'

And that was what they were doing now—relaxing together and feeding each other sweetmeats from the brass tray at their feet, as they lay stretched out on the big, silk-covered divan. Except that Amber's remark about his having lied to her had just caused Zoltan to pause in mid-bite and blink at her.

She looked back at him, unrepentant. 'Yes, *habibi*,

you lied to me. And don't try to deny it. I've seen the evidence with my own eyes.'

Zoltan scowled a mock scowl and gave her a small squeeze. 'That's a serious accusation. You'd better explain,' he demanded.

Amber smiled. 'You told me women weren't allowed to use the library. You said that was why I had to work in the courtyard. Well, it just so happens that when I was on my way to your office earlier I passed through the library, and what do you think I saw?'

He laughed, clearly knowing very well what she was about to say. 'I've no idea,' he teased. 'What did you see?'

'I saw a woman in one of the study booths, that's what I saw, looking very much at home there, too, I might add.' She growled and accused him, 'You deliberately deceived me. You made that up, didn't you, just to force me to work in the courtyard?'

'I had to. I'm sorry—' he started to apologise. But, before he could say more, Amber silenced him with a kiss.

'I ought to have known.' She hugged him and held him. 'I ought to have realised you wouldn't allow a rule like that.' He was a good man. A fair man. She was very sure of that. No wonder she was so utterly, helplessly in love with him.

'It was my fault you believed it, but there'll be no more deceptions from now on. No more secrets. No more mysteries. I promise you that.'

He kissed her and held her in the circle of his arms. 'You're part of me now. We're part of each other. Nothing must ever come between us again.'

For a long time, they just sat there embracing one

another, listening to each other's heartbeats, drinking in
each other's scents, lost in their new happiness and in
the wonderful love they shared. Then, suddenly, glancing down at her, Zoltan kissed her and said, 'I thought
you were going to try calling your mother again?'

Amber had been thinking the same thing. She smiled
at him. 'You're right.' And she reached for the phone
that lay on the floor by the divan, pressed the redial
button and listened as it began to ring. 'Let's hope she's
in this time,' she said.

Her mother answered almost at once.

'I got your fax,' Amber told her. As she spoke, she
snuggled back into Zoltan's warm arms. 'And now I'm
phoning to tell you were absolutely right. The reason
I'm staying on is a very special man.'

As Zoltan laughed, she kissed him. 'A very, very
special man.

'Now sit down and make yourself comfortable,' she
instructed her mother. 'I'm going to tell you all about
how wonderful he is and it may take some time. . .'

MILLS & BOON

Next Month's Romances

♡

Each month you can choose from a wide variety of romance novels from Mills & Boon. Below are the new titles to look out for next month from the Presents and Enchanted series.

Presents™

CRAVING JAMIE	Emma Darcy
THE SECRET WIFE	Lynne Graham
WEDDING DAZE	Diana Hamilton
KISS AND TELL	Sharon Kendrick
MARRYING THE ENEMY!	Elizabeth Power
THE UNEXPECTED CHILD	Kate Walker
WEDDING-NIGHT BABY	Kim Lawrence
UNGENTLEMANLY BEHAVIOUR	Margaret Mayo

Enchanted™

THE SECOND BRIDE	Catherine George
HIS BROTHER'S CHILD	Lucy Gordon
THE BADLANDS BRIDE	Rebecca Winters
NEEDED: ONE DAD	Jeanne Allan
THE THREE-YEAR ITCH	Liz Fielding
FALLING FOR THE BOSS	Laura Martin
THE BACHELOR PRINCE	Debbie Macomber
A RANCH, A RING AND EVERYTHING	Val Daniels

KEEPING COUNT

How would you like to win a year's supply of Mills & Boon® books? Well you can and they're FREE! Simply complete the competition below and send it to us by 31st October 1997. The first five correct entries picked after the closing date will each win a year's subscription to the Mills & Boon series of their choice. What could be easier?

$$6 + 3 + \boxed{} = 14$$

$$\boxed{} + 2 + \boxed{} = 15$$

$$\boxed{} + 1 + \boxed{} = 16$$

$$\boxed{} + 6 + \boxed{} = 17$$

$$\boxed{} + 3 + \boxed{} = 18$$

$$\boxed{} + 1 + \boxed{} = 19$$

$$\boxed{} + 5 + \boxed{} = 20$$

C7D

PLEASE TURN OVER FOR DETAILS OF HOW TO ENTER ☞

How to enter...

There are six sets of numbers overleaf. When the first empty box has the correct number filled into it, then that set of three numbers will add up to 14. All you have to do, is figure out what the missing number of each of the other five sets are so that the answer to each will be as shown. The first number of each set of three will be the last number of the set before. Good Luck!

When you have filled in all the missing numbers don't forget to fill in your name and address in the space provided and tick the Mills & Boon® series you would like to receive if you are a winner. Then simply pop this page into an envelope (you don't even need a stamp) and post it today. Hurry, competition ends 31st October 1997.

Mills & Boon 'Keeping Count' Competition
FREEPOST, Croydon, Surrey, CR9 3WZ

Eire readers send competition to PO Box 4546, Dublin 24

Please tick the series you would like to receive if you are a winner

Presents™ ❏   Enchanted™ ❏   Temptation® ❏
Medical Romance™ ❏   Historical Romance™ ❏

Are you a Reader Service Subscriber?   Yes ❏   No ❏

Ms/Mrs/Miss/Mr_____

(BLOCK CAPS PLEASE)

Address _____

_____

_____ Postcode _____

(I am over 18 years of age)

C7D